AF660175

PRAISE FOR THE BOOK

"Simply put, I endorse him. Can I say any more than that?"

—JAY ABRAHAM, FOUNDER AND CEO OF THE ABRAHAM GROUP

"There are those who talk a good talk, and then there is Steve, who lives it."

—JIM KWIK, *NYT* BESTSELLING AUTHOR OF *LIMITLESS*

"Steve Sims dares to imagine achieving the impossible and then delivers time and time again. Better still, he has distilled his trade secrets into this compelling book that has its own audacious goal to teach you how you can achieve almost anything you can imagine, regardless of the odds or incredulity of your friends, family, or others who find your ambitions too threatening to their own limiting beliefs of what is possible."

—ROLAND FRASIER, CO-FOUNDER OF SCALABLE, DIGITALMARKETER, AND TRAFFIC & CONVERSION SUMMIT

"The day before something is a breakthrough, it's a crazy idea. Steve Sims has the ability to go after goals that most laugh at, and that's usually just before he achieves them!"

—PETER H. DIAMANDIS, MD, FOUNDER OF XPRIZE AND SINGULARITY AND AUTHOR OF *ABUNDANCE* AND *BOLD*

"Almost no person on this planet has made the kind of impact to my thinking as Steve Sims. He taught me how to lean into big, 'stupid' goals and watch how magically they don't seem so stupid after crushing them."

—BRANDON TURNER, FOUNDER OF OPEN DOOR CAPITAL AND FORMER HOST OF *BIGGERPOCKETS PODCAST*

"If you need something done or something that is impossible, Steve is your man. He gets it all done."

—TUCKER MAX, AUTHOR, SPEAKER, AND FOUNDER OF SCRIBE MEDIA

"In a 'gotcha' society where people are scared to try, Steve stands out as someone who aims high and achieves higher. We need more Steve Sims in the world if we wish to change it, and this book sets you on the right route!"

—JOE POLISH, FOUNDER OF GENIUS NETWORK AND GENIUS RECOVERY AND AUTHOR OF *CREATIVE CAREERS: MAKING A LIVING WITH YOUR IDEAS*

"In a world filled with constraints (both real and imagined), quite often people are more afraid of being laughed at than they are of missing out on their big dreams. Steve demonstrates how if your goal isn't laughable, then it's not big enough!"

—JJ VIRGIN, CELEBRITY NUTRITION AND FITNESS EXPERT AND FOUR-TIME *NYT* BESTSELLING AUTHOR

"Full transparency: I know Steve, so I know where other people see 'stupid,' Steve sees opportunity. Steve starts where others give up. He succeeds where others are afraid they'll fail. He is also generous. He wants others to succeed too. He demystifies the mysterious and gives practical how-to advice on how to reach your goals. Reading Steve's book is like talking to him; he is clear and a hell of a lot of fun. Go for Stupid. It's a smart move."

—JEFFREY MADOFF, CEO OF MADOFF PRODUCTIONS, KEYNOTE SPEAKER, AND BESTSELLING AUTHOR OF *CREATIVE CAREERS: MAKING A LIVING WITH YOUR IDEAS*

GO FOR STUPID

GO FOR STUPID

The Art of Achieving Ridiculous Goals

STEVE D. SIMS

MANJUL
Manjul Publishing House

First published in India by

MANJUL

Manjul Publishing House Pvt. Ltd.
• C-16, Sector 3, Noida, Uttar Pradesh 201301 – India
Website: www.manjulindia.com
Registered Office:
• 10, Nishat Colony, Bhopal 462 003 – India

Go For Stupid © 2022 Steve D Sims.

Original English language edition published
by House of Nomad SOC, USA.

Arranged via Licensor's Agent: DropCap Inc.

All rights reserved.

Go For Stupid- The Art of Achieving Ridiculous Goals

This edition first published in India in 2023

All rights reserved

ISBN 978-93-5543-315-2

Printed and bound in India by Manipal Technologies Limited

This book has been published with all reasonable efforts taken to make the material error-free. While all attempts have been made to verify the information provided in this publication, neither the author nor the publisher assumes any responsibility for errors, omissions, or misuse of the subject matter contained in the book.

All rights reserved. No part of this book may be used or reproduced, stored in or introduced into a retrieval system, or transmitted, in any form, or by any means (electronic, mechanical, photocopying, recording or otherwise) without the prior written permission of the Publisher. Any person who does any unauthorized act in relation to this publication may be liable to criminal prosecution and civil claims for damages.

Saying thank you seems inadequate when the person you are thanking is your everything.

This five-foot-five beauty scares and excites me at the same time, and without her, I wouldn't be the person I am today.

To you, Clare, I can only say I love you, and I hope to show you every day how much you mean to me, but for now: thank you!

CONTENTS

INTRODUCTION 15

1. I ASKED 21
2. IT'S ALL DONE FOR YOU 33
3. THE THREE KEYS TO A SUCCESS MINDSET 43
4. LIKE BUYING A DIET BOOK TO LOSE WEIGHT 57
5. THEY ALWAYS LAUGH BEFORE THEY APPLAUD 63
6. DO YOU HAVE STANDARDS? 79
7. DO YOU HAVE A KENNETH? 91
8. DON'T SELL THE ITEM, SELL THE REACTION 99
9. AMAZONIFICATION 121
10. LET'S PLAY A GAME 137
11. GOING FOR STUPID: IT'S NOTHING NEW 159
12. CHALLENGE THEIR WHY 167

CONCLUSION 181

ACKNOWLEDGMENTS 187

Before you read this book, please scan this QR code for a personal message from Steve.

INTRODUCTION

In 2017, I wrote the book *Bluefishing: The Art of Making Things Happen* to challenge myself. I never thought I'd be an author. Once it came out, I was blown away—really, just floored—by the response that it received: it was translated into six languages, and I received emails, tweets, DMs, and letters from people around the planet about it.

But what shocked me more than the compliments was how many intelligent people told me, "I could have never done that." When I dug deeper into why they thought that, the response was always the same—it wasn't that they doubted their ability to achieve it, but that they were afraid to look "stupid" if they failed. They cared too much about what other people would think of them, people who were watching what they did for the sole purpose of laughing at them. Thanks to today's "gotcha" society, people are terrified to do anything that may get them ridiculed.

Talking to these people, I realised that I have a superpower: I have never cared about anyone laughing at me.

My wife tells me it's like I've always worn blinders (those screens they put on the eyes of racehorses so they can't see anywhere but forward). I could never see or hear the hecklers around me because I was laser-focused on my goals: having a conversation with this successful person, getting that person on stage, putting together dinner in a museum. It wasn't until I started to slow down and revel in the connections I had made that I realised that there are some people out there that love to ridicule anyone who dares to try. Even more astounding, I realised there are people who cared what these hecklers thought about them. I was staggered.

When I was still working in the concierge business, for every event I was asked to plan, my first thought was, *How far can I take this? What would make this a stupid achievement?*

One of my favourite go-for-stupid moments was helping a client, Dan, become the shortest-term lead singer of the rock band Journey. When he first came to me, he told me he wanted to meet Journey backstage at one of their concerts so he could tell them how he used to perform their songs in a cover band, which earned him enough money to get his degree, which, in turn, set him up for success. He wanted to thank them for creating music that got him through his toughest days. They were the soundtrack to the movie of his life.

With so much passion and gratitude radiating from Dan as he told me his story, I was surprised he was willing to settle for a simple handshake and three-minute conversation. That's what he wanted for the crescendo of his movie? I decided to see how far I could take this request. I communicated with the band and got Dan on stage to sing four songs with them at a concert in San Diego. (You can read the entire story in *Bluefishing*.)

I wanted to be laughed at. I went for stupid. And that has led to enormous success and served as a critical foundation for every future venture.

I see too many business owners and entrepreneurs who are working harder, not smarter. They're close to the action rather than *in* the action where they want to be. If only they'd take some stupid chances, but their fear of ridicule stops them.

You might not want to admit it, but you are full of fear: fear of failure, sure, but fear of being laughed at and embarrassing yourself and maybe your family. You're worried about the wrong fear. You should be afraid of staying still because you never try. Fear just getting by or settling because you aren't willing to go for stupid.

Let me ask you a question: what would you be able to achieve if you didn't care about being laughed at?

WHAT YOU'LL LEARN

Reading this book will give you an unfair advantage over your competition. Putting the actions into practice will remove the pain and fear of being laughed at. When you're done with this book, you'll no longer overthink your fears. You'll go for stupid, ridiculous goals—and achieve them. You'll no longer be constrained by a "gotcha" society.

To be more precise, you'll learn:

- How to see opportunities everywhere
- The three keys successful people live by
- The importance of mindset
- Why your standards should be constantly upgraded
- How to avoid Amazonification
- Why it's not all about you
- Examples of the most famous stupid goals in history
- The importance of asking why

At the end of each chapter are three questions to ask yourself. Use the provided space to answer them honestly and act on any discoveries that reveal themselves.

Most importantly, you'll learn that going for stupid is the best way to achieve ridiculous goals.

MORE "I CAN" THAN "IQ"

You may be reading this book because you read my first book, *Bluefishing*. (If you are, welcome back!) *Bluefishing* was all about sharing how you can break down any door, transform your life, and achieve the impossible.

Throughout my life, I have always moved with purpose and impact. Jay Abraham, an American business executive, conference speaker, author, and friend, once said that I have a greater "I can" than "IQ." I have never used the word "impossible," and that resulted in a business with a client list of the world's rich and famous, many of whom have become close friends. However, as you'll learn in this book, we need to constantly grow in our lives and businesses. My concierge firm taught me many life lessons that I was able to share in my first book, but it was eventually time to move on to the next challenge.

Since *Bluefishing*, I have created a personal brand (SteveD-Sims.com), a membership community (SimsDistillery.com), a marketing and branding company (Sims.Media), and a reverse mastermind company (SimsSpeakeasy.com). (You'll get to hear about Sims.Media and Sims Speakeasy later in this book—including the time I took a court judge to a brothel.) The one thing every one of these ventures has in common is being stupid. No, the businesses aren't stupid, but with the creation of each one, I went for stupid even though there were many people who told me they were bad ideas. (People were astounded I was starting a business during a pandemic.)

I learned how to go for stupid the hard way, and now I'm sharing those lessons with you. Be warned: in this book, I tell the truth the only way I'm willing to: directly, boldly, and without holding back. You won't find any fluff or "feel good" motivations in these pages. This is about creating practical actions to produce astounding results. In a gotcha society, this book will yell at you to ignore what everyone else thinks and go for big, stupid, ridiculous goals. After all, if a bricklayer from South London can do it, you can too.

A last caveat for you. This book isn't meant to be read and put aside. You need to use the information and take action. If you aren't going to do that, you might as well not read it. This is not a book to sit on your coffee table to impress visitors. It's a guide to help you achieve your wildest dreams.

Let's get started.

CHAPTER ONE

I ASKED

It's Sunday, September 28, 2014. I was sitting at an iron table in the garden restaurant of the Hotel de Russie, Rome, when a client called.

"Steve, I know you're in Italy. I want you to do something for me."

"Of course," I said. "What do you need?"

"I'll be in Florence this Wednesday with my fiancée, her mother and father, and a friend. I need you to sort out a fantastic dining experience for me. Something extraordinary that shows how creative, connected, and powerful I am. Can you do it?"

"Absolutely."

On Monday, I jumped on the train and headed to Florence.

I started work as soon as the train arrived at the station. By Tuesday afternoon, everything was set for Wednesday night.

At nine o'clock in the evening, a white horse-drawn carriage trots through the Piazza della Repubblica and stops in front of the Hotel Savoy. Our group of six exits the hotel and climbs into the carriage.

The horses clip-clop through the cobblestone streets, over Ponte Vecchio, past the Uffizi Gallery, through the Palazzo Vecchio, and alongside the Duomo. Finally, the coachman steers the carriage up a side street.

On this side street, they approach a set of oversized wooden doors. Abruptly, my client yells out, "Stop!"

The carriage jerks to a halt, jostling the group. The client leaps out, dashes over to the doors, and starts hammering on them with his fist.

Bang, bang, bang!

It's nine o'clock at night. The stars are out, and everyone's shutters are closed. Contrary to many Mediterranean cultures, this city goes to bed early "at eight thirty."

Bang, bang, bang!

His fiancée is half out of her seat, hand raised. "Hey, hey, hey," she said, voice low. "You'll wake people up. Don't do that."

He replies, "You don't get it. In here is Michelangelo's *David*."

He is pounding on the side doors to the world-famous Accademia Gallery.

"We go home tomorrow. If I knock on this door long enough, security or a cleaner or someone will open it up. I'll slip them ten grand, and they'll let us wander around David for a while."

Bang, bang, bang!

He's still hitting the door. The sound is now echoing up and down the street. His soon-to-be mother- and father-in-law look at each other. They're thinking they have a psychopath coming into the family.

Bang, bang, ba—

The doors crack slightly. A moment later, they open fully to reveal a red carpet that stretches down the corridor all the way to the foot of *David.*

In front of *David* is a candlelit dinner table set for six.

Of course, a dinner party wouldn't be complete without music. And an extraordinary dinner deserves the best. As their first course is served, Andrea Bocelli walks out to serenade the group.

It was a phenomenal night. The client was pleased. The fiancée was awestruck. The in-laws were impressed. While I will never forget this event, it's not because of the meal, the music, the setting, or the client's happiness.

This was a pivotal moment in my career, in my life, and in

my mindset. A lot of people know I pulled this off. I've told this story before, on stages, on podcasts, and in my book *Bluefishing*.

However, most people don't know the rest of the story.

LEARNING THE MOST VALUABLE LESSON

Monday, on the train ride up to Florence, I made calls to powerful people. When you're in a room with powerful people, powerful things happen. And these were people who could get me into the place I wanted.

They agreed to close down the Accademia Gallery at three o'clock in the afternoon on Wednesday so I could set up the dinner party. Once I had gone through the formality of drinking too much espresso and shaking hands, they passed me over to a curator. They said, "We're going to make this a fantastic night. He's going to look after you. Anything you need, you just ask him, and he'll get it sorted for you."

I'm thinking, *This is smooth. It's only taken me half a day to get an entire museum shut down.*

I'm pretty full of myself by now.

I turned to the curator and said, "We've got the chef with all of his equipment coming at 6:30 p.m., so we need the side doors open. He'll set up in the courtyard. Is that alright?"

The curator crossed his arms and replied with a thick Italian accent, "That should be okay."

It wasn't the enthusiastic yes I was looking for, but fine. I went on. "The piano that Andrea's son will play is coming at 7:00 p.m., so we'll need the back doors open and security ready. Is that okay?"

Arms still crossed, he said, "I'll see what I can do."

Fine. "Andrea is going to turn up at 7:30 p.m. I need the front door opened up and security tight so that when the car turns up, he can get in before anyone sees him." If you're in Italy, the two biggest VIPs are Andrea and the Pope, and we didn't want a crowd outside.

He gave a small shrug and said, "It shouldn't be a problem."

I'm getting aggravated at this point, but I had work to do.

Wednesday evening rolls around, and I'm standing with Andrea's wife, Veronica. Their son is tuning the piano while Andrea warms up his tonsils. After a few bars, Andrea decides he doesn't like the reverb, so he makes the staff move the piano to a different location.

The entire room is made of marble. It's not the best place for acoustics. The son tunes it, presses a few keys, Andrea warbles a bit—not right. They move it again, tune it, press a few keys, sing—not right.

Veronica and I watch as the piano dances around the room in search of the perfect spot.

After a few minutes, Veronica excuses herself to talk to Andrea, who is a perfectionist that can't find the perfect spot. To my right, the curator is leaning up against the wall.

Now, there's something you need to know about me. Something that I've always been very up-front about.

I am an immature child.

I've never been accused of being mature, and I certainly wasn't that night. This guy had annoyed me, so I decided I was going to teach him a lesson. I was going to show him that he needed to treat people with a little more respect (and by people, I meant me).

I called out, "Hey, Luigi, come here!" His name was not Luigi.

He casually walks over to stand next to me. I'm five foot eleven, 240 pounds, and wearing a black shirt and jeans. Luigi is five foot eight at most, maybe 140 pounds soaking wet, and wearing a tailored jacket, embroidered waistcoat, and fancy pocket square, looking every inch the dapper Italian man.

"What do you think of that table?" I asked him.

"It is wonderful. It is beautiful. It is amazing."

"Look at that view. You're about to have dinner, and that's your view. Can it get any better than that?"

"No," he said in his Italian accent. "It is phenomenal. It is wonderful."

I continued. "You're having that meal, with that view, and then Andrea Bocelli starts to serenade you while you're chewing your meatballs. Does it get any better than that?"

"No. It is incredible. It is fantastical."

I brought it home: "So let me ask you this. How come I managed to pull it off?" I expected him to say, "Well, no one's as connected as you, Steve." "No one's as smooth as you." "No one's as good-looking as you." Any one of those would have pandered to my ego, and I would have been fine.

He looked up at me and said, "No one's ever asked."

I crumbled, hands on my knees, breathing out a word that's not fit for print. When I stood back up, this tiny Italian man was looking up at me with a huge, cheeky grin. He knew he had gotten me.

I may be immature, but I know when I've been beaten. We went out for dinner after the event, ate some steak, drank a few cocktails, and had some laughs. In fact, we've been friends ever since. I still jokingly refer to him as Luigi.

But that moment changed my life forever.

The next day, I flew back to Rome, where I was retained to get a couple married by the Pope (you can read all about it in *Bluefishing*), before heading home to LA.

On the plane ride, I wrote down a list of the most significant feats I'd accomplished for my clients: playing drums with Guns N' Roses, singing on stage with Journey, walk-on roles in movies, sitting front row at fashion week, diving to see the Titanic. Over the next three months, I reached out to every single one of the people I had dealt with. I asked them the same question I had asked Luigi: "How did I manage to pull this off?" There wasn't a single variation on the answer.

"You asked."

There's a famous quote you might have heard of by Wayne Gretzky: "You always miss 100 per cent of the shots you don't take." I learned I needed to ask more of my relationships. Ask more of my family. Ask more of my business partners. And most importantly, ask more of myself.

This was one of the biggest turning points in my life. I had been so stupid that I had failed to be intimidated. So many people are held back in life because we live in a gotcha society.

THE FEAR OF LAUGHTER

People today love to laugh at others. We're in a point, stare, and giggle society. We love to gawk at people when they get smacked in the face, fall off a ladder, or slip on the ice.

We are naturally programmed today to laugh at people's missteps. The result is that we're now scared of doing anything. Not because we're afraid of failing—we're afraid of being seen failing.

A few years ago, I was at a nearby shopping mall with my wife.

We had just exited Target and were heading to the Starbucks that was a few stores away. In front of us were two men, who were walking slower than I expected. I glanced around them and saw why.

In front of them was one of the largest women I've ever seen in my life. I looked at her and was amazed for two reasons.

First was her upper body strength. She had her arms held out like tree branches with at least four bags on each side. Second was her pigheadedness. Because she was holding her arms wide, no one could get past her. She was taking up too much room, so we were all forced to walk at her pace.

As I was thinking about how impressed I was by her strength and her ignorance, she tripped. And because her arms were stretched wide and weighed down, she had no way to protect herself.

I dropped my wife's hand and lunged for her. The two men in front of me grabbed for her. None of us got there in time, and she fell hard. The sound of her face slamming against the concrete floor was like dropping a thick piece of steak on your kitchen floor.

After a moment, she started to roll over awkwardly onto her back, before slowly sitting up. Her legs were splayed, and there was a huge red mark down the right side of her face. Her shopping bags had flung off her arms, and the contents were scattered everywhere.

The guys and my wife crouched down to check on her while

I scrambled around on the floor to grab all of her items. I put everything back in the bags and placed the bags between her legs where they'd be safe.

We stayed with her while she waited for the mall's emergency services to arrive. I noticed that as my wife talked to her, the woman kept darting glances left and right, up and down. I assumed she was looking for a bag that I had missed, so I said, "All of your bags are right here. This is everything I could find."

Before she fell, there were only a handful of people milling around. Now there was a large crowd, all staring at her. She kept looking around, so I asked, "Is there anything I didn't get for you? I can look for it."

She glanced down at the bags but quickly returned to looking around. Then she said quietly, "No, no. I just don't want anyone to have recorded that."

This woman would wake up in the morning with a bruised face if she was lucky or with some broken bones if not, but she wasn't worried about that. A swollen face was not the worst-case scenario in her mind.

She was terrified that someone had taken a video and that she would end up being laughed at on the internet. "A large woman fell over. Ha, ha, ha."

This is the society we live in. We love to laugh at people, no matter the situation.

When Elon Musk revealed his Cybertruck, no one cared about

the feat of engineering. This truck was utterly unique in every aspect, from the wheels to the doors to the mechanics. All they did was laugh because the steel ball he threw cracked the bulletproof glass.

The video he released a few days later showing his team throwing multiple steel balls at the same time repeatedly without even the smallest crack? No one cared. They only watched when they could point and laugh at a man who dared to do something different.

Everyone has said or done something stupid in their life. (Twenty years ago, we all definitely said and did something stupid.) But today, people are terrified to do or say anything when a few words can be cherry-picked and used in a sound bite to ridicule us.

Our gotcha society has destroyed our ability to communicate, relate, and connect to each other.

LEARNING MY LESSONS

Luigi taught me the necessity of asking. The fall revealed I was ignorant of the fear of laughter. I had been—and still am—too stupid to care.

As a child, I would constantly ask for a lollipop before dinner. Who doesn't want their dessert first? Every time, my mother would tell me no. But as a child, I wasn't deterred. I was curious and wanted to see what I could get. It took Luigi smacking me with the obvious that I was still daring to ask like a five-year-old.

After talking to Luigi, the managers for Guns N' Roses and Journey, the producers for fashion week, and the custodian for the Titanic, the secret to my success became crystal clear. I started to question what else I had achieved simply because I had dared to ask and wasn't afraid to try. What other opportunities did I—and could I—create by going for stupid?

GO FOR STUPID

Ask yourself these three questions and answer them in the space below.

1. What is the stupidest goal for yourself that you can dream up?

....

2. What did your five-year-old self dare to ask for?

....

3. What have you done that people laughed at before you achieved it?

....

CHAPTER TWO

IT'S ALL DONE FOR YOU

Like many entrepreneurs, my early path was a series of aggravations, mistakes, and ill-qualified work. I would choose jobs that surrounded me with affluent people in order to become a by-product of the room I was in. Of course, I failed at all of them. But failure is an education in what not to do. I learned what jobs I was not a fit for—in fact, I became very educated.

One of these educational experiences led me to an understanding that changed my life.

I landed a job as a trainee stockbroker with a company that moved me to Hong Kong. I had no experience or qualifications, something they clearly overlooked. However, I had to start doing the job, and it only took them a few days to realise I had no idea what I was doing and fire me.

Now I was trying to find a job in a foreign country, and my only qualification was to lay bricks. Building companies in Hong Kong didn't need a British bricklayer, considering the cost of manual labour was remarkably cheap in Asia.

Finally, I was able to get a job as a doorman for a nightclub. (My appearance paid off for once.)

I remember standing outside the door with the other meatheads, thinking to myself, *I've reached the lowest point. I went from the noble profession of bricklaying to being a thug for hire.* I was the big, scary guy on the door. My entire job description was to deter violence between patrons and slap people around if they weren't paying attention to the rules. No one wants to do that. (Well, I'm sure there are some people that want to do it, but I certainly didn't.)

However, I was an entrepreneur at heart, and we have a special mindset. We don't see things the way other people see things. We see opportunity. We notice trends, styles, changes, requirements: often, if it annoys us, we find a solution, and then we find someone else who has the same problem and invoice them.

I realised that by being at the door, I was getting a beautiful view of society, psychology, and human nature. It was a free masterclass—actually, I was getting paid to learn.

When my mindset shifted, I became physically excited to work the door. I was filled with childlike energy, bounding up the alley every night. The other doormen would exchange glances and ask me, "What are you so excited about?"

There are people who get into jobs for the pay cheque, and there are people who get into jobs for growth. I had originally gotten into this job for the pay cheque, but now my eyes were open to the idea I could also get immense growth as well. That is what was so exciting to me.

Every night I went to work and watched how affluent people interacted with each other—and how people who were *pretending* to be affluent interacted with each other.

I became extremely knowledgeable in body language. I knew at a glance which guys were trying to hide the fact they had already had a few and were looking for trouble. I could see through the fake flirtation to get in the door free of charge. I knew which girl packs were looking to start a fight because they thought it was funny.

This superpower let me turn away the people who were just going to cause trouble. But I didn't stop there. I also declined regulars if the club was having an off night.

CONTROL THE DOOR

When I first started doing it, my boss would yell at me: "What are you doing?" I kept telling him, "Look, we want them to come back again. I guarantee they'll come back to me tomorrow and ask me if it's a good night." They always did, and when it was a good night, I'd let them in.

After a while, I wanted to become more than the meathead at the door.

Tell me if this sounds familiar: you're sitting in a restaurant, and you see the manager floating from table to table saying, "Hey, is everything okay? You having a good night?" I started playing this role every time I was on duty inside the club. (Again, my manager tried to check me without success.)

I was looking for any way to connect with people.

To my managers, I was a weird irritation that they couldn't put their finger on. I was eliminating fights (my "real" job), making people feel comfortable, and engaging them. I was the thug on the door, *and* I was the manager making sure everyone was okay. The real manager couldn't fire me because I wasn't doing anything bad, not to mention the number of fights had gone down drastically since I started controlling the front door.

My process was simple: I only let the right people in the door because I wanted to communicate with them inside.

Forty years later, I'm still the doorman.

Everything I do, whether it be an exclusive speakeasy, a coaching program, or a speaking gig, I control the door. Who do I want in my life? Who do I want in my circle? Who do I want in my training room?

I spend more time focusing on the people I let in the door than I do about the cheques they are writing to me. You can always make more money, but it only takes one bad egg to lose all the others. When that happens, you don't just lose that client, you lose the entire room.

It's a twist on the old Jay-Z 99 problems: if you focus on who walks through your front door, you've removed 99 per cent of the problems once they're inside.

PASSWORDS

While I was controlling the door, I started giving out passwords to use the next day. (That's how the title *Bluefish* came to be.) When I turned away regulars because it wasn't a good night, I'd tell them, "Come back tomorrow and give me XYZ password, and I'll let you in."

This sounds trivial and really stupid—and it absolutely is. But imagine: ten people are lined up in front of you, and you've challenged them to tell you one of the characters from the *Teletubbies*. After some smirks and laughs, one of them says, "Tinky Winky," and you let the group in.

One day, after doing this for a few weeks, a bartender came up to me—and I would love to tell you I was a genius and this was completely planned, but it wasn't—and said, "Do you know, everyone who walks into the club is already smiling."

Of course they were. They had just had to say a silly name in front of their friends. Imagine if everyone that walked in your front door came in with a wide smile. I thought, *Well, yeah. They're going to the club to have a few drinks, listen to great music, and pull a beautiful girl. They're already in a state of excitement.*

I decided to put it to the test. I went to other nightclubs in the area, got a whiskey, and stood by the front door as people came in to watch their faces. Not a single one was smiling.

As soon as they walked in, they would start scoping out the room, figuring out what was going on and who was there. There was always an undercurrent of nervousness: *what's the night going to be like?*

They were trying to quickly gauge the temperature of the room. Now imagine if everyone walking into the club was already smiling. What's the temperature of that room going to be like? To find out, I had my fellow meatheads take passwords for a night, and then I stood inside the club doors and watched people come in.

Everyone came in giggling and smiling because the girlfriend or wife or group of macho guys had to say something ridiculous, like purple octopus or butter fudge nut. I watched them come in, and then quickly turned to view the rest of the room—and found that it was like they were welcoming the newcomers in.

7-38-55

You've probably heard the saying, "Misery attracts misery"—and it absolutely does. But so does happiness.

Dr. Albert Mehranian, a professor at UCLA, created the idea of the 7-38-55 rule (though it was popularised by Chris Voss in his book *Never Split the Difference*). This rule states that:

- 7 per cent of the communication we have comes across in the copy, i.e., the words, the text, the message
- 38 per cent of it comes across in tonality
- 55 per cent of the communication comes over in our body language, our visual symbols, our signs

There have been dozens of studies done about the contagiousness of laughter, but the one you've probably seen is the video of a man on a train. This man is sitting by the door in a crowded compartment when he starts giggling. Then, he starts chuckling, and before long, he's howling laughing, tears in his eyes. However, the video doesn't focus on him—it's focused on the surrounding train-goers. It starts with the people closest to him, who begin to smile and then giggle. Before long, the entire compartment is either smiling, at a minimum, or fully laughing along.

These people have no idea why the man started laughing in the first place, but they can't help themselves. No joke was relayed, and there was no explanation of what he saw. They were taken in by his body movements, his tone, his laughter, and his facial expressions. Humans are attracted to humour. We are attracted to people who are smiling.

So while misery may attract misery, happiness also attracts happiness. When you attract happiness, you remove obstacles and open up opportunities—people are much more open when they are experiencing childlike glee.

I learned three things from controlling the front door:

1. Fights virtually stopped.
2. More people waited in long lines to get into the club because everyone wanted to be in a room with happy people.
3. People became more accepting.

THE YELLOW CAR EXPERIENCE

There's an experience I call the yellow car situation. (It has a fancy name—Baader–Meinhof phenomenon—but that's a mouthful.)

I bet this has happened to you. You're in a conversation with someone, and they ask you, "What do you think of my new car?" You look out the window at the hideous thing and say, "It's nice. I've never seen that shade of yellow before." The conversation continues, but then, for the next few days, the only car colour you see is that hideous shade of yellow.

If you open your mind to opportunities—like seeing a shade of yellow—the only thing you can see during the day is opportunities. I saw an opportunity at the club, took a gamble on it, and began to see opportunities everywhere.

WAS THIS DONE FOR ME?

Dr. Sean Stephenson, an American therapist, self-help author, and motivational speaker, used to ask himself a single question every time something good or bad happened: "Was this done for me or to me?" He would categorise every situation based on those parameters.

Of course, when something bad happens, your first instinct is to say, "That was done *to* me." But was it? Or was it done to challenge you? The more you categorise situations, the more accepting you'll become that most things are done for your benefit.

Being a doorman was done for me. I can say with 100 per

cent certainty that I would not be where I am today, rubbing shoulders with the people I am, speaking at the events I am, creating the events I am, if I did not learn so much about human nature working that door. I truly believe that people want to keep their eyes open to opportunity. But to do that, you have to be open to looking at every situation as being done for you rather than to you.

Once you've accepted everything is done for you, you gain the ability to differentiate, control, and compartmentalise every single situation you find yourself in. Like a hideous yellow car, you'll find that most of life is done for you.

GO FOR STUPID

Ask yourself these three questions and answer them in the space below.

1. When was the last time you evaluated who you allowed through your front door?

....

2. What was the biggest challenge that happened in your life that you now realise was done for you?

....

3. Name a situation you're in now that is challenging that, if you were to reframe it, you would see as a benefit.

....

CHAPTER THREE

THE THREE KEYS TO A SUCCESS MINDSET

One of my main goals as a doorman was to be able to personally interview and converse with the powerful, successful people who came to the club. If I was trying to do this today, I would have just started a podcast, but as podcasts didn't exist in the nineties, I had to find a different way to grab the attention of the people I wanted to learn from.

I may not be much of a social butterfly (if you need to find me at an event, check the corner nearest the bar), but I knew how to get people what they wanted. I would get these successful people whatever they needed for the night, such as a meeting with their favourite rockstar or a business icon, or simply into a party they were not invited to. The next day, I'd be able to phone them and ask, "Hey, did you enjoy yourself?" When they said yes (and they always did), I would hit them with a very important question.

However, I learned early on that if you don't like the answer, it's because you're not asking the right question. This knowledge came to me in the form of some very uncomfortable moments. When I started having these conversations, I would begin by warming them up, usually by validating that they got to do what they did because of me. Then, I would hit them with, "Oh, by the way, I always wanted to ask you this: how come you're rich and I'm not?"

That was a very, very bad question. If you ask about "rich," a person's first thought is how much money is in their bank account and portfolio. The fact is it wasn't valuable information for me. It's not something most good people like talking about, making it an awkward question. Every time I asked it, I was met with hesitation, resistance, and friction. After a few times, I realised I was wasting my opportunity by asking for it.

The next time I had the opportunity to speak to someone, I tweaked my question. After all, if you don't like the answer, ask a different question. This time, I asked: "How come you're wealthy and I'm not?" While this was a much better question, I received terrible answers: "I found God." "I found the church." "I met my wife, got married, and had kids." I would think, *I'm not going to go to your church and marry your wife. This isn't helping me.* I understand how their mind looks at these things as wealth, but I couldn't replicate that.

Once again, I didn't like the answer, so I changed my question for the third time—and it was a home run. "How come you're successful and I'm not?" This was the right question because now they were giving me the mindset that led to their success. I could absorb, change, and follow that mindset before I even left the table. I took their knowledge and changed how I looked at the world.

I decided to take it one step further. Now that I had the right question, I went on a mission to ask that question to as many people as possible.

The most important aspect of this was that I started using the information they gave me right away. What kind of moron would I be if I took their knowledge, said "Thank you very much," and then didn't implement it in my life? By utilizing their wisdom, I was able to tweak my home run question one last time: "How come you're successful and so many other people are not?" I wasn't including myself anymore because I was applying the learnings to my life.

After asking dozens of incredibly successful people this question, I noticed some repetition in the answers. There were three things that successful people did differently from non-successful people. (Let's be honest, there are probably twenty-five different things, but these were the three most common answers that came up every single time.)

THE FIRST KEY: RELATIONSHIPS

The first thing I learned is that successful people value relationships. This was a weird one for me to learn because when I was growing up, I would hear rich people say: "Yes, let's talk about it over drinks." "We can discuss over a round of golf." "Let's do that over brunch." You start to think, *Oh, that's what rich people do. I don't need to do that.*

However, I learned that successful people don't get into deals or opportunities with people—they get into them with culture. Let me explain.

As long as the person that they were talking to or exploring an opportunity with shared the same values, standards, commitments, and beliefs, everything else could be taught.

If you weren't great at putting together a spreadsheet, but you had the same values, standards, and beliefs *and* a great idea? They could get someone else to put it into the right format. That was an easy fix.

Successful people employed and partnered with others based on their culture keys. If you take on people based on the deal, the money, or the chequebook, instead of the culture, you'll never connect. There will be a time limit on that relationship because friction will always exist when your thoughts and cultural beliefs are not aligned.

Affluent people value relationships differently: anything you're weak on, you can be educated on—if the right foundations are there. Imagine if you have a sandbox and everyone in it is culturally aligned to your values, beliefs, and goals. How powerful would that sandpit be?

THE SECOND KEY: CURIOSITY

The second difference was curiosity. Successful people are endlessly curious. They love to find out how things are done: "Why does it have to be done that way?"

The most successful people are five-year-olds at heart. They take nothing for granted. They never think, "Well, it's always been that way, so that's how it has to work."

I've talked to many moderately successful people about their marketing over the years. My first question is usually "How do you do marketing?" followed by "How long have you been doing it like that?"

"Twenty-five years," they answer.

"Why don't you change it up?"

"Because that's how we've always done it."

The truly successful person is the one that says, "*Why* does it have to be like that?" Why can't I have a lollipop? Why can't we do it this way? Why can't we play like this? They gamify business—they literally make it fun.

Think about a puzzle. Typically, those two pieces are supposed to fit like this...but do they have to? Maybe with a little bit of jimmying and a hammer, they could fit differently and create an even better pattern.

Affluent people become five-year-olds, questioning everything. We're told as we grow up that our answer is wrong if it doesn't fit in a certain box. But look at all of the entrepreneurs out there who are crushing it by doing everything "wrong." If we followed only what we were taught, we wouldn't have computers, electric cars, civilian space travel, the light bulb, or even coffee. Nothing great in this life would exist if those creators had listened to the people terrified to creatively disrupt the status quo.

THE THIRD, AND MOST IMPORTANT, KEY: TIME

I've met with thousands of successful people over the years and received thousands of answers. They've all helped me, steered me, and made me the man I am today.

However, the one that's still important—and has, in fact, become more valuable over the years—is the last key difference: how successful people relate to time.

Successful people view time differently than everyone else. They knew they could make more money. They knew they could make an impact. What they could never, ever do is generate more time. They couldn't order it on Amazon or build it in a factory. It was a rarity, an exclusivity. They only had a certain amount of it, and they didn't even get to know when it would run out.

When you have a conversation with a successful person, they have zero interest in what you recently watched on Netflix. They are uninterested in what you had for breakfast. They care about what you're working on, what impact that's going to create, how it will help them, and how it will help other people.

I've had conversations with some of the most powerful people on the planet, and every time, those conversations feel like interrogations: Why you? How are you going to do that? How's that going to work? Why do you think you're the one that can do it? What's the impact? What's the by-product? It's like being interviewed by the Gestapo.

The reason is that they value time more. They don't want to waste it on water cooler conversation. They want to know what you are doing with your time, what they can potentially do to be a part of it, and what you can do to help create an impact with that time.

Think about how much you value time in your everyday life. Are you using it to build impact or binge Netflix?

Affluent people can make more money. They can create more impact. But they don't have any control—no one has any control—over time. Consequently, they are exceptionally careful with how they spend it.

When I was younger, I'd spend my time walking around the mall or lounging on the sofa watching TV. However, when COVID arrived in the US with a bang and turned everyone's lives upside down, I asked myself, "Was this done for me or to me?" This was a statement that my friend, the late but always great Dr. Sean Stephenson used to say a lot. I suddenly had the one thing successful people are desperate to have: more time.

I no longer had to travel for work. I didn't have to drive anywhere. I didn't spend hours in line at the airport. It was like I was gift-wrapped more hours in a day. I didn't even have to go to the store because Instacart and Amazon would deliver anything I needed.

At the same time, half of the planet was texting each other or posting on Facebook, "What are you watching on Netflix? I'm binge-watching everything." Instead, I asked myself, "What can I create? What can I disrupt? What problem can I solve?"

Did you know that more than five million people became millionaires across the world in 2020?[1]

How is that possible, you ask? Because successful people used their newfound extra time to analyse what they were doing, what the impact of it was, and whether or not it was working. If not, they used the opportunity to pivot.

So many companies had to pivot to keep your attention. The companies that pivoted successfully saw their profits skyrocket. One of the earliest pivots—and this is truly ridiculous—was Domino's Pizza.

Pre-COVID, if you were going out for pizza with the family, I'm going to guess that Domino's was pretty low on your list of fine-dining pizza joints. But at 10:00 p.m. on a Friday night after a ball game or a couple of beers with the guys, you'd get the munchies and Domino's delivered. As soon as COVID lockdowns started happening, Domino's launched an advertising campaign saying, "Don't worry. We'll come to you and leave it at your door."

Everyone thought that was genius. Of course, it's what they had always done, but now they were pointing it out and to great success—they made a fortune with that campaign. Every other pizza manufacturer on the planet, any other pizza com-

1 "Millions Become Millionaires during Covid Pandemic." 2021. BBC News. BBC News. June 23, 2021. https://www.bbc.com/news/business-57575077.

pany you can think of, does the exact same thing. Domino's just made it obvious.

The biggest blessing I had was having a time-focused mindset before COVID came along. My mindset was the reason that I was able to think, *I have a double day now.* I had more hours in the day, and I used them to go for stupid.

THE SMARTEST PERSON IN THE ROOM

I knew I wasn't the smartest person in the room. That was never in question. But it was also never a concern for me when I was talking to these affluent people because as dumb as I was, I was never dumb enough not to listen to advice from someone who had what I wanted.

I would sit there and literally have an "aha" moment. And when I stood up, I felt taller because I was now carrying that intelligence. Each time, I would think, *This is how I'm going to react now.*

Once I nailed my question and received incredibly helpful information, there was only one thing left to do: utilise it.

In the early stages, my mindset would consider, "What would Kevin do? What would Robin do? What would Mark do?" I metaphorically put myself in their shoes, which is different from emulating fake it 'til you make it. Pretending has no reaction—it's superficial. "Look at me. I'm leaning against this expensive car." Great...did that work? Are you wealthy now?

When you emulate a person, your thought process changes.

If they wanted that car, what steps would they take to get it? If you want to become a successful person, the first step is to replicate them in your mindset.

Put yourself in their shoes and adopt their mindset—even if you don't know them personally. If you have a challenge in your life, you can think, *What would Elon Musk do?* He would play the game.

People today don't play enough games. "I can't get to the person I want to get to. I can't scale my business." Ask yourself what your most-admired successful person would do in your situation. Go for stupid, prepared to be laughed at, and try it anyway. That's what they would do.

Plus, if it fails, you'll now be educated on what doesn't work, so you can try again, but smarter.

CHANGING YOUR MINDSET

Over and over, I'd repeat to myself, *How would a successful person handle this situation?* You can't purchase your mindset on Amazon. What you can do, which is much more beautiful, is change it while you are sitting in your chair. You can change it right now while you are reading this book. When you finish this sentence, you can tell yourself, "From now on, I'm going to value every minute as though it's my last. I'm going to look at every relationship I have and determine if we have cultural alignment. I'm going to enter every opportunity with overflowing curiosity."

Changing my mindset allowed me to react differently than

the herd, which in turn allowed me to create incredible experiences for my clients. These conversations were a learning point and a confirmation of how I should act. The client stories were the by-products of this change of mindset.

When you're growing up, you want to be rich. No eighteen-year-old says, "I want to be wealthy" or "I want to be successful." They literally say, "I want to be rich." What they mean is they want to make a million dollars. They think, *If I could be a millionaire, it'll always be sunny. The world will be mine, and I'll always be driving red Ferraris with a hot trophy wife on my arm.*

This is a great vision—until you make a million.

Then you realise you're still tight for money. You *might* be able to afford a toilet in Manhattan with one million bucks. Maybe. I doubt it. If you have kids in private school, you absolutely cannot live in Manhattan as a millionaire. It's not financially possible.

The trouble with only caring about a dollar amount is that you have to constantly adapt, edit, and tweak your goal posts.

Focusing on money can be scary because when you reach that number, it's easy to fall into depression when you realise that you're still struggling to pay school fees even though you netted seven figures. That's a terrifying feeling.

But, if you focus on a success mindset, your by-product is freedom thanks to a constantly full bank account. One doesn't come without the other.

Change your mindset, change your world.

A NOTE ON CHOOSING THE RIGHT QUESTION

To know what the right question is, you first have to ask all of the questions. Remember back in grade school when the teacher asked, "Does anyone have a question?" We were all too scared to raise our hands—except for little Susie in the front row, who was on her tenth question, irritating the teacher and becoming the target of our spitballs. This just taught her—and us—that the outcome of asking too many questions was annoying people and getting wet paper stuck in your hair.

However, this is the opposite of how it should be. Today, we don't ask enough questions. If you don't ask questions, you won't learn the difference between a wrong question and a right question. And if we don't ask the right questions, we are going to be doomed to make mistakes based on bad information.

Most of our problems today, whether it be religion, war, race, riots, police brutality, etc., are all because of bad communication. We need to take a step back and begin asking as many questions as required until we hit on the right question that leads to the answer to the problem we have.

A trick I've learned from asking the wrong questions is to reverse into the right question.

I liken it to starting with the crescendo of the movie and then writing backwards. Say I want to ask Elon Musk how he raised $10 million when he was still a nobody. I need to ask a question that leads him down a rabbit hole to a burrow containing the answer I need.

A lot of people think the purpose of a question is to initiate a conversation. They're wrong. The point of a question is to get the answer that satisfies your question. Questions like, "How's your day going?" "What have you been watching on Netflix?" "How's it going?" These are wasteful questions—and remember, successful people don't waste time.

Reverse into your question. What answer are you looking for? Then tailor the question to get that answer—and make sure it's both short and clear. "How did you make $2 million last month?" "How did you go from PayPal into space exploration?" The reason your question needs brevity is to ensure a lack of confusion.

"I wanted to ask you, well you know, back when you were at your last company, when you were doing XYZ, what did you think about..." You lost me. I have no idea what you are trying to ask. I don't want to hear about the life history of where I was. I want to know what your question is.

Be crystal clear in what you are asking to dictate the answer you want to receive.

Just know that learning to ask the right clear, concise questions takes trial and error. Failure is a great educator. And when you find the right question, be sure to remember 7-38-55. Your body language, facial expressions, and tonality will all play an even greater part of creating the right question than the words you use. If you are in a person's face, they're not going to want to talk to you, no matter how well-worded your question is. (If you need a refresher on 7-38-55, head back to Chapter Two.)

GO FOR STUPID

Ask yourself these three questions and answer them in the space below.

1. What are you wasting time on today?

....

2. What are the three things you'll change your perception on?

....

3. What relationships are you spending your time on?

....

CHAPTER FOUR

LIKE BUYING A DIET BOOK TO LOSE WEIGHT

Asking the right question is only the first step. Often, we focus on the outcome as the answer, when, in reality, it's the by-product of the answer.

When I speak at events or training sessions, I frequently ask the audience, "Who has ever gotten skinny by buying a diet book?" I then follow it up with, "Or who has gotten money from buying a book on finances?"

Every time, a few people put their hands up. I'm always happy they do because it gives me someone I can pick on. I pick one of them out and challenge them: "Did you really?"

It causes everyone in the room to rethink, especially when I push the point home: "As you were paying for that book at your local Barnes & Noble, shoved it in a bag, and walked out of the door, were the pounds dripping off of you?" The answer is always no because you don't lose weight simply by buying the diet book. Likewise, you don't get richer by buying a book on money or fitter by buying a fitness magazine.

You get all of those things as a reaction to the action.

ACTION VS. REACTION

What you do creates a reaction. People focus on the reaction as what they need to do, but that's the wrong mindset. A great painting won't magically appear on your living room wall. You won't suddenly have a million dollars in your bank account. You won't immediately be slim without putting the action into it.

The reaction is the goal, and the action is the workload. It's the strategy, the techniques, the graph.

Imagine creating a meal for a group of people. Too many people don't look at the ingredients of the meal and then wonder why the end result tastes horrible. They didn't focus on the intricacies—the freshness of the vegetables, the expiration date on the sauce. They didn't pay attention to the steps they were supposed to take or the correct order—boiling the water before you put in the rice.

It always stuns me when people state their reaction—I want to be rich, I want to be a world-class speaker, I want to be an entertainer, I want to be an A-list actor—without realising that's the destination, not the route. Yes, you need to know where you want to end up, but then you need to reverse engineer your route.

When we're kids, our goal is to have more toys or sweets or presents. As you get older, you still want things, but those things change. No forty-year-old man wants another lollipop, but he may want a new car.

Your goal changes based on your experience, age, and priorities in life. Every goal is valid, but you need to understand that it's the reaction, it's the destination. Whether you want a slimmer body, greater finances, a better company, or stronger relationships within your business, you need to take the reaction and reverse engineer the route by asking a simple question: what action do I need to take in order to get there?

That action is what you need to focus on. Stop focusing on the reaction. Have one, put it up on your vision board. Then focus on creating—and then following—the roadmap to that reaction, not the little picture taped to your wall.

KNOW YOUR REACTION

If you know that the goal is the reaction to an action, then you need to realise that the first step to getting that reaction is to change your mindset.

As you learned in the previous chapter, when I asked the right question of successful people, I became smarter just by sitting in a chair. While my bank account wasn't increasing and I wasn't losing weight by listening to them, my mindset was becoming educated on what I needed to do.

A popular saying I love goes like this: "Little hinges swing big doors." If you can change your mindset a millimetre, then an inch, then a foot, then a yard, you can get closer to your goal. But it all starts in that moment when you're sitting in a chair and saying, "I am going to stop eating fatty food. I am going to stop listening to Barry at the end of the bar for my financial advice. I am going to examine my relationships."

You become smarter sitting in the chair, and the second you stand up, that's your first action. You want something now, and you are actioning towards it. The by-product will be accumulation, but it always starts with the mindset.

I learned from successful people to think, *Okay, I want to be wealthy, so I have to do this because the reaction will be money. I want to be fitter and healthier, so I need to work out three times a week because the reaction will be health.*

It's essential that you understand when you ask yourself a question and begin looking for an answer if the answer you find is actually the action or the reaction. Understanding this distinction has made me challenge the way I ask questions.

I know now that if I want better answers, I have to ask better questions. Today, I have people that I want to do business with—I want them to work with me—but I haven't yet found the right question to ask them. And until I do, I'm not going to waste an opportunity or burn a bridge by asking a substandard question.

However, you have to learn what the right question is through experience.

GO FOR STUPID

Ask yourself these three questions and answer them in the space below.

1. What are your three current goals?

....

2. Identify the first step you need to take for each of those three goals.

....

3. What is your timeline to achieve each goal?

....

CHAPTER FIVE

THEY ALWAYS LAUGH BEFORE THEY APPLAUD

It's 2014. I was contacted by Peter Diamandis, who asked me to put on an experience for sixty of the most affluent and powerful people in the world to tour the best technology companies in California. I set up tours of Tesla, the spaceport where Richard Branson's Virgin Galactic was, the Burton's Scaled Composites (which was the actual spacecraft that Richard Branson purchased to start Virgin Galactic), and the early stages of AI with Fox.

The pinnacle element of this entire day trip, however, was taking the group to SpaceX to meet Elon Musk himself.

The day of the SpaceX tour came long, and I had luxury buses pick up the clients outside of their various hotels. We drove down to SpaceX, which is located in Hawthorne, near downtown LA, just outside of a small private airstrip. Once inside, they received a private tour of SpaceX's factory. If you're wondering what the inside of SpaceX looks like, you don't have to. In the first Iron Man movie, there's a scene where Tony walks through his factory—that's SpaceX. In fact, Marvel gave the company one of the Iron Man costumes, which now has a place of pride next to the reception desk.

Along with the factory, the clients were given a tour of all the nonconfidential areas, including the main communication room filled with computer screens that looked like a miniature Houston. Once the tour was complete, the group waited in one of the central meeting areas while I went to fetch Elon for his talk.

Among the group were a couple of my regular clients to whom I wanted to give an extra special treat. I subtly pulled them aside and said, "I'm going to go pick up Elon now. Do you want to come with me?" Of course, they both gave an enthusiastic yes. Who wouldn't want essentially one-on-one time with one of the most powerful people alive?

About halfway through the facility, we ran into Elon, who had already started to head our way. I introduced him to my two clients, and we all started walking back the way we came, where Elon would talk about the company, answer some questions, and take some pictures—the usual glad-handing things.

The hallways we were travelling down were large enough that the four of us could walk side-by-side. Elon was on my right, and to my left was one of the clients. This guy was over the moon that he was walking through SpaceX with Elon Musk himself—he didn't say a single word the entire walk. He had a huge grin on his face, chuffed to know that he was going to walk into the room with Elon Musk. That was all the validation he needed.

The client on my furthest left: chatterbox. Nerves and excitement had gotten to him, and he started firing four million questions at Elon, who is *not* a chatterbox. Like most affluent people, he doesn't care what you ate for dinner or what you recently binged on Netflix. He had no interest in answering this guy's questions.

Unfortunately, the client had a goal to get a reaction out of Elon in order to get a conversation going with him. It got to the point that I started thinking I was going to have to give the guy a poke in the ribs to get him to calm down. It would have been uncomfortable because, to do so, I was going to have to lean over the other client.

As this thought crosses my mind, the client leans across us and says, "So Elon, how do you feel about the fact that NASA publicly laughs and ridicules everything you do with civilian space exploration?" This tour was happening during a period of time when NASA had created a team to rebut every single thing Elon said about space on Twitter. They were literally trying to publicly humiliate him by saying, "There's no room for you in space exploration. That sounds good in theory, but this is no place for amateurs." Some of their remarks were, simply put, cruel.

It was the only time Elon responded to this client. Without even looking at him, Elon said, "They will always laugh at you just before they applaud."

That was it. Full statement. It shut my client right up, but more important than that, it was a holy grail moment for me. We reached the rest of the group, and Elon spoke as planned and took photographs with everyone. But my mind was repeating that one sentence over and over. I'll remember it forever.

This was a man who was focused on a goal. He knew, without a shadow of a doubt, that any ridicule and humiliation was just a few feet away from a standing ovation. He understood that if people were laughing at him, then he was onto something.

Today, we're in a world where people are terrified, not of failing, but of people laughing at them.

THE UNTOLD STORY

I've talked about that life-changing sentence from Elon Musk at several events. But I haven't talked about the rest of that tour.

Some of our other destinations included Silicon Valley headquarters, such as Facebook, Instagram, and Microsoft, which was our first stop.

The first thing you notice when you walk into Microsoft is that every single wall is curved. (Imagine trying to walk around there with a couple of drinks in you.) The reason there are no straight walls is because "nothing is straight and narrow." Great analogy, but not the coolest part of the tour.

As we walked through the building, we got to go into all these different rooms with the latest—often unseen—technology.

Some of it was so top secret that we weren't allowed to bring our phones in with us.

Then, we moved up to the second floor. In the middle of the space, it was like the builders took a break and forgot to come back. There was a mid-sized room, four walls all filled with mismatched windows, and a door with a padlock. Our guide unlocked the door and ushered us in. It looked like a junk store. The walls were unpainted, and cables and computer parts were tossed on shelving units that looked like they were from Bed, Bath, and Beyond.

The rest of the headquarters was so clean it was clinical. This room had wires, cables, bolts, tools, hard drives—anything remotely related to computers was tossed in there. If it wasn't for the fact that on the mismatched, scratched-up desks, items were being built, I would have put money on the fact it was a junk store.

I turned to our guide and asked, "What is this place?"

"This is our garage."

I'm sorry, what? He saw my face and explained further: "There's no one from Silicon Valley that didn't start in their garage. In a garage, no one could see what you were doing, so if something failed, no one cared. We have about thirty garages on campus." He pointed up to a sign above the door that said, "Garage 12."

"If you want to build something, you get the padlock to reserve the room. Once you're inside, this is your place to screw up.

If it happens to work, you bring it out to the main rooms, and it gets polished."

I was gobsmacked. I couldn't get over the idea that Microsoft, with all of its billions, had a place to openly fail—a place where you could try new things and no one would laugh. This felt monumental to me.

When we toured the Instagram campus a few days later, I noticed a garage door on the side of one of the buildings. I asked our guide what was in there, expecting to see some electronic scooters. He opened it up, and guess what? It was another junkyard, just like the one at Microsoft, that employees could "rent."

When you've been developing new ideas in a garage and succeed, you get benefits like a shiny, clean operations room. This results in a loss of that mojo, that creative spark that led to your original great idea. What Microsoft, Instagram, and I'm sure other companies have figured out, it helps their employees' creativity to have a space where you have to physically bolt parts in, where the floor is wonky, the chairs are ugly, and the tables are beat up. It makes them feel comfortable—at ease enough to try things with no one to laugh at your failure.

I hope everyone is secure enough to risk being laughed at before they're applauded. But imagine if you could work on something that no one else knows about and no one could judge. What could you achieve in that situation? Look at what Microsoft and Instagram have created.

LEAN INTO FAILURE

Elon Musk has a childlike genius—and like a child, he believes anything can happen. When you combine belief and action, the result is, unsurprisingly, success.

Elon is always gamifying, asking, "How could we do this?" He's never looked at a problem as something to solve. He's never looked at making an existing thing better. He always starts with, "Why aren't we doing that?"

Often people are annoyed when they have to replace the squeaky wheel of the wheelbarrow—that they don't use. Elon doesn't focus on the wheelbarrow at all. Instead, he asks why it's required in the first place and then looks into changing *that*.

When he decided to work on civilian space exploration, Elon used this philosophy for several aspects of the launches. One dealt with the fact that the original fuselage was built on the West Coast but launched on the East Coast. (You'd think that they'd be made next to the place they're going to be launched, but no.)

Instead, they would load the fuselage onto a boat, float them through the Panama Canal, up the coast of Florida, and then unload them at the harbour. Moving something so heavy so far costs millions and millions of dollars. However, Elon realised that if he could shrink the diameter by mere feet, he could just pop it onto a truck and drive it across the country. Then he'd be paying significantly less.

He took action and used increases in technology that provided more power in thinner frames and was able to reduce the overall size of the fuselage without reducing the interior. He gamified it: how do we get from A to B cheaper?

A second way he gamified space exploration was by looking into what makes launches so expensive. He found that when you break down the costs, one of the biggest factors was the two giant fuel cells that attach to the side of the rocket in order to launch it into space.

However, once the rocket is past the earth's gravitational field, they are ejected off. Nine times out of ten, they land in the ocean and sink. But again, with the simplicity of a child, he gamified it at what some people considered an immature level. His thought was, *If we get those back, refuel them, and bolt them back on again, we can save hundreds of millions of dollars.*

When you think in a childlike fashion such as this, the question becomes, "Okay, I know what the end goal is. How do I get there?" You already know the answer. You already have the result. You need the structure, format, and route, which is less complicated than you think. If you know where you are going to end up, you can backtrack to where you are now: this creates your roadmap.

And that's exactly what he did. He knew the end goal was to safely land them, refuel them, and reattach them to the next rocket. Now, how would he get them down? Didn't know. How would he get them to land in the right spot? Didn't know. Those elements didn't matter at first because he knew what the end goal had to be.

He took action with small steps. First, they would detach cleanly from the side of the rocket, and then they would land on a floating pad in the ocean. Keep in mind these cells were travelling a hundred thousand miles an hour before peeling off and, through the use of gyroscopes and GPS, would land on a pad that was floating in the ocean, moving with the waves. Just to be able to land anywhere near that pad would be an amazing achievement.

Elon managed, with pinpoint accuracy, to land those cells on the pad. In the early days, if it wobbled even a little when it landed, it would tip over and explode like a Hollywood action movie. The evening news loved to report it.

However, I was able to be in the room with Elon and his team in those early days. I was standing in the back with a few other guests, and everyone in the room was glued to the giant screens. The fuel cell came down and started to land, but the afterburners, which were there to keep it stable, started to taper off because it looked settled. Then, as if in slow motion, it started to tip over and BANG—it blew up.

Every single screen was focused on that cell, and so every single screen showed the massive explosion. I'll never forget that moment because every person standing in the back, including me, covered our mouths, gasped, and leaned back.

Every single person on that team, including Elon, leaned in.

Unsuccessful people shy away from a problem: "Oh my God, it's all going wrong." Successful people lean into a problem:

"Where did it go wrong? What did I learn from this moment? What can I do differently next time?"

The fuel cells exploded on the landing pad quite a few times. But ask yourself, when was the last time you saw or heard about a fuel cell explosion on the news? I'm guessing you're going to say a few years. How many times has SpaceX gone up and down in those years? Quite a few.

The reason you no longer hear about the fuel cells is because they work. Things that work don't make for good airtime. "Oh, it landed. Goodie, he did it right." No one cares. Today's society would much rather see it explode so they could point and laugh: "He just lost a hundred million dollars!" If it bleeds, it leads.

Elon wasn't fazed by the laughter. He leaned into the problem to see where the education was.

You don't become successful from success. You become successful from the mistakes. They are the true education. Repeat that, and it becomes experience. Repeat experience, and it becomes credibility. And credibility is something you can invoice for.

BUT YOU CAN'T DO EVERYTHING YOURSELF

One of the downsides of being an entrepreneur at heart is that we try to do everything. Yet, one piece of information I learned is that smart entrepreneurs realise that they should only do what they're good at and then recruit other people to do what they're not.

I also learned that the number one reason many entrepreneurs go bankrupt—and this is a truly ridiculous statement to have to say—is because they become successful.

That sounds like an oxymoron, but let me explain. Imagine you are really good at making and painting pots. In fact, you make the most amazing pots on the market. You're exceptionally good at sitting at your wheel with your clay, painting incredible designs, and setting the kiln to just the right setting. Now everyone wants one of your pots.

What happens next is your downfall. You have to get involved in fulfilment. You have to start advertising. You need to set up invoicing. You need to handle promotion, website design, social media, customer funnels, and all the things that come with a business. You're great at making a pot—but that doesn't mean you're great at fulfilment, invoicing, payroll, or accounting.

Entrepreneurs end up having to do all the parts of running a business that they can't do because the one thing they can do is in demand. The smartest thing an entrepreneur can do is recruit their weaknesses.

You need a mindset that understands that you do what you can do and rent the ones you can't. Once you get people to do the business basics you can't do, you get to exponentially grow the amount of your extraordinary. This is when the secret pill of stupidity really comes out to play.

SET STUPID GOALS

If you have a goal to make $2 million this year, and you think that's a ridiculous, sexy, crazy goal, then you need to make it $10 million. Fail, and you achieve $5 million.

You see, goals are target points. I hate to say it, but most of the time we don't actually hit our goals. We fall slightly short. "I want this body." "I want to buy that car." But along the way, a different car becomes available, and along the way, a party has to be attended. We live in an imperfect world, so most goals are never fully achieved.

I'm a great believer that if you know that not all goals are achieved, then you need to make your goals stupid, ridiculous, and laughable.

You want to be 180 pounds, so make your goal 170 pounds. If you fail, you'll still be at 175 pounds. You want a house on a beach but fail, yet you still get a house that's walking distance to the ocean. In order to achieve what you want, you have to aim for what is stupid.

In Chapter Eleven, we'll talk about people who have done exactly that: gone for stupid, ridiculous goals that everyone laughed at until they were applauding. Sometimes the by-product of a preposterous goal is better than reaching it.

For instance, Coca-Cola was originally created as a way to help calm an upset stomach, and now it's the most popular soft drink on the planet. The creator wanted it to be a medicine. They were looking to have it sold in pharmacies. Their goal was to create something to help with digestion. They ended up with a multibillion-dollar soft drink. Coca-Cola is one of, if not the, most famous brands on the planet. They failed successfully.

This book started with my story of getting Andrea Bocelli to serenade my client at a famous museum. My go-for-stupid goal was, "Well, if I don't get Andrea Bocelli, maybe I can get someone who is just excellent to come sing for us." I went for stupid comfortably expecting to get less than. But with practice, you end up getting exactly what you aim for.

FUTURISTS

Some of the biggest brands on the planet have made going for stupid an actual job. There's now a job title at big-name companies called a futurist.

A futurist is someone whose job is to dream up the way we will live, act, and work decades in the future. After all, if you can visualise it, you can create a roadmap to it.

One of my favourite examples of this is of a gentleman by the name of Ray Kurzweil. He filmed a documentary called Transcendent Man, where he tried to work out how many parts of a human being can be replicated by technology before it stops being a human being. (To be clear, this is not the Johnny Depp movie called *Transcendent Man*.) If you want to mess with your head, dig up this old documentary and give it a watch.

Ray Kurzweil predicted that we wouldn't need buttons to text and communicate with others. Instead, we'd have an in-hand AI system, which he named Siri. Yes, Ray actually invented Siri before there was technology to support it. He invented Siri before Apple purchased a license for it, and now Siri is one of the most successful AI systems in the world. Of course, before long, everyone was copying the idea, and Alexa came along.

However, going for stupid doesn't mean you have to book a museum every time you want to host a private dinner party. It's about how you interact with everyone and everything. You need to look at things differently than anyone else.

CONSTANT AND CONSISTENT GROWTH

A good friend of mine, Joe Polish, once told me, "The definition of hell is to meet the man or woman you could have become." It stopped me in my tracks.

By now, you should understand that you have to ask the right question, think differently, then take action, all while ignoring the laughs. However, every time you follow this template, you need to grow a little bit more.

I was always terrified of not having constant and consistent growth, but I never realised that I was the one challenging myself to grow—or as my wife used to say, that I was a dog with a bone—until Joe said those words to me. He made me realise that I always took every opportunity that came my way.

Now, when you're sixty-five, you should quantify the benefit of each opportunity before you take it. But when you are in the early stages of your life and career, try everything. Entrepreneurs are taught not to be yes people (because that's usually what gets them in trouble), but I disagree. I've always focused on trying to make sure there are more yeses in my life than nos.

For instance, I took the opportunity to write a second book. And just like when I wrote my first book, it's been a horrible experience. I'm sure some people love writing books, but for me it's an uncomfortable, awful, frightening process. The dumbest part is that writing this book was worse than writing my first book because the first time, I didn't know what to expect.

Now that I've gone through the process once, I know what mistakes to attempt to avoid replicating, but I also know how impactful and powerful a book can be to my career. *Bluefishing* catapulted me from a career in concierge services into whatever you call me now. I don't know what this book is going to do, which is terrifying. But I am not the guy who wants to live with the risk of not trying. This book may fail, fall flat on its face, and be laughed at and ridiculed, which I can admit is not what I want out of it, but at least it'll be a wealth of education.

As we get older, we lose the ability of curiosity. When we're kids, we are endlessly curious. "What happens if I push this button?" We take apart clocks just to see how they work (and then deal with angry moms when we can't put them back together). Then one day, we're told two magic-killing words: "Grow up." We stop getting curious; we stop trying to see how things work.

But I never did. I ignored everyone who told me to grow up, and it's my curiosity and ability to try something different that allows me to fail, become educated, and grow.

I challenge you to action your goals. If the you from five years ago met you today, would they be proud of your growth, or would they be disappointed? When I first start working with new coaching clients, I have them create an action plan. One month in, I asked them how it's going, knowing they've done absolutely nothing yet. I have them write down all their excuses, and then talk them through what they can do to conquer each one.

Ask any one of them, and they'll tell you I am very blunt in my follow-ups. But it's because I know how many people have a great idea that they're still talking about five years later, having not taken a single step towards making it a reality. Never forget that there will eventually be a five-year time that comes up where you can no longer do what you want to do.

GO FOR STUPID

Ask yourself these three questions and answer them in the space below.

1. What's your stupid goal?

....

2. Name three things you're frightened to try.

....

3. What are you going to do today so in five more years, you aren't in the same place?

....

CHAPTER SIX

DO YOU HAVE STANDARDS?

A close friend was flying into town for a meeting, and we met for a drink. And because I'm a great friend, I arranged a little surprise: a private tour of the Warner Brothers movie lot. We got to walk around the sound stages, and I introduced him to some of the big names I knew who were on set that day.

After the tour, we went for a quick bite and drinks at the Smokehouse, a very old steakhouse that's located across the street from the giant Warner Brothers gates. It's been there since before the movie lot was created. Clark Gable, John Wayne, Clint Eastwood, Ocean's Eleven: anyone you can think of in the entertainment world has, at some point in their career, walked through the doors of the Smokehouse. It's an iconic place that seems to shout stories at you from the moment you step inside.

Now, I'm not saying it serves the best food in the world, but who doesn't want to eat at a legendary restaurant, especially when you might see a big-name movie star walk in? We walked in, took a seat at the bar, and ordered a few small snacks. I rode my motorcycle to the lot to meet my friend, so I wasn't having any alcohol (I had to drive home, after all).

He said, "I'm getting picked up by an Uber, so I'm going to have an old fashioned in your honour."

I'm known for loving an old fashioned cocktail. It's always my drink of choice. It has four ingredients: a good bourbon, a good syrup mixture, an orange peel, and a large ice cube. Done. That's the entire old fashioned. There aren't a lot of ingredients in that, so you'd think it wouldn't be hard to mess it up. But the number of times people get it wrong is incredible—they'll give it to me in a funny glass, or worse, they'll deliver it with a massive half a lump of orange in there like it's a Jamba Juice or full with shards of ice so that it's diluted before it even gets to you.

When my drink is made wrong, I always say, "Excuse me, this isn't an old fashioned. You need to remake this." I will send it back every single time. Often, the people I'm with mock me for doing it, but understand: my standards start at that drink.

I told my friend to knock himself out. He ordered an old fashioned—keep in mind, this is not a fantastic cocktail bar—and they delivered him the worst version you can get of this drink: half a lump of orange and loads of ice, like it was a Coke from McDonald's.

He looks down at the drink, and I look at his face. He slides it closer, leaving a trail of condensation from all the ice, and I'm still looking at him. He glances at me, picks it up, takes a sip, and promptly puts it back down. Cocking an eyebrow, I asked, "Well?" He shrugged and replied, "I've had better."

"So what are you going to do?" I asked.

"I'm only having one drink, and I'm going to go."

"Oh, okay. So you're going to drink *that* drink?"

"Yeah, I was thinking of drinking this drink."

"Right. Just understand that what you do in the next ten seconds dictates your level of acceptance. Your standards are going to be defined by your reaction to this."

With that statement hanging in the air, he waved over to the bartender and said, "Excuse me. Do you have another bar staff here that can make an actual old fashioned? This isn't really how it should be done." The bartender was very apologetic. "I'm so sorry. We've got a new guy on today. I'll go make you a new one myself." He came back with a superb old fashioned made exactly as it should be.

You don't have to be rude—my friend certainly wasn't—and you don't have to be spending a lot of money. But even if you order a plain hamburger and fries, and those fries are lukewarm at best, you need to ask for a fresh plate. Your standards are set by the smallest action. If you are willing to settle for a poorly made drink that you paid for, what else are you willing to settle for?

CONSTANTLY UPGRADE YOUR STANDARDS

As entrepreneurs, we grow and scale, and as we do so, we want to have our eyes opened to new opportunities, possibilities, and perspectives. We talked in Chapter Two about seeing something everywhere once your eyes have been opened to it, such as yellow cars and opportunities. The same can be said of your standards.

One of my cornerstones is a constant yearning and unacceptance of anything lower than the standard I'm currently at. When I was first starting out and buying jeans, I would only buy Levi's jeans because, in my eyes, that was the best brand I could get at that time—until I would find another brand that was even better than Levi's. Then, I would no longer settle for Levi's jeans because my standard had increased.

There are a lot of standards that will grow as you become more successful as an entrepreneur. You find a bigger office space, bigger monitors, the latest phone technology—we're constantly upgrading to keep up with the next standard. That's great, but it's not enough. We also need to do this with our education.

I've been a member of many organisations that have held countless events. More times than I can count, I have gone to an event, and by noon, I've left the event and gone home because that room didn't challenge me. I've even received complaints because I've left early, and while I mean no offence, I'm in my late fifties. I'm not getting any younger or any prettier—I have no time to waste.

My standards tell me that I need a room to challenge me. I need my environment to challenge me. There's a common saying, "If you're the smartest person in the room, you're in the wrong room." You need to increase your standards and go to a room that challenges you in order to grow.

RELATIONSHIPS

Entrepreneurs especially have a blind spot when it comes to upgrading: relationships. While they will upgrade their car, their house, their watch, their clothing—constantly developing greater taste buds—they neglect their relationships. They strive to gain access to anything they've never had before. Yet, they'll look at their partner and think, *Eh, you're an anchor to a past that I have left*. You should demand more of your relationships. You don't have to change your partner out for a new model, but demand that they (and you) be a better spouse.

For a relationship to outlast upgrades, both people have to be equally unaccepting of low standards. In 2022, I'll be celebrating thirty-seven years with my wife. I'd love to say it's because I'm so wonderful, I'm built like a stallion, and all these macho things, but the fact of the matter is that I've never settled for anything—and neither has she. She won't settle for a man that won't take care of and be there for his family. She won't settle for a home that is less than what she wants. When we got married, we didn't realise that this alignment even existed. To be honest, it sounds like something that would cause stress and panic: "Oh God, what if I don't meet their standards in the future?" But it doesn't for us because we both yearn for the same high standards in every aspect of our lives. "There's a scuff on the car. Let's get it repaired because I'm not going to drive around in something substandard." Our relationship works because our level of standards is aligned.

I'm not saying that you need to suddenly start looking at your relationship and asking, "Hey, is this the right relationship for me?" Before you do that, you have to look at the relationship you have with yourself, and you have to look at the standards that you carry.

When you've assessed the standards you have, and you commit to living by those standards, only then can you look at the people around you and decide: Do they share the same cultural keys? Do they share the same beliefs? And do they share the same standards as you? After you answer these questions, you can decide if you need to cut and run or if you can work on that relationship. You'll often find that if you increase your standards, the people who are meant to be around you will do the same. If they don't, it's time to say bye, whether it's your wife, girlfriend, partner, husband, boyfriend, or best friend. If they don't want to raise their standards, you need to let them go.

However, don't just ditch someone because they are an anchor of a memory or a trigger to your past. We should all be attached to our past. It's where we came from, and we can't know where we're going until we know where we came from. Being an anchor is not necessarily a bad thing in your relationship. Riffs happen if they're still stuck in the same standards as when you first met.

Imagine if you met someone in 1985, and in 2022, they were still wearing the same clothes with the same haircut and refused to change them. You may have outgrown that person.

Like I said before, relationships are hard for most but are hellishly difficult with entrepreneurs, especially when you have an attitude of *I'm not settling for anything. I want to buy this, but I can't afford it, so I'll wait and buy the best rather than buying this and settling.* It's a slippery, slippery slope.

THE PRICE TAG DOESN'T DICTATE YOUR STANDARDS

Many of you reading this are probably thinking, *Sure, it's easy to say, "I'm going to fly first class instead of economy" because you've got the wallet for it, Steve.* I'm here to tell you that standards don't have to start with a big price tag.

You can ask any of my kids or family members, and they'll tell you that I've been notorious for sticking to standards my entire life. My kids grew up embarrassed to go to any restaurant with me. In fact, one of my kids would always say they had to go to the toilet as soon as the server began to lead us to our table. I only found out a few years ago why. If our server led us to a table that was near the kitchen or restrooms, or if it was a table and not a booth, I'd immediately say, "I'm sorry. I don't want this table. I'll take that table." My son, to avoid the embarrassment of me forcing our server to take us to a different table, would go to the bathroom even though he didn't need to. He didn't want to "bounce around" to different tables until I was satisfied.

However, he's since learned that standards apply to even something as low-level, and price-tag-free, as making sure you get the right table.

Set your standards, and stick to them. Two things will happen: your expectations of what you deserve will grow, and your acceptance of other people's standards diminishes because they now have to rise to your level.

People are attracted to your level of commitment to your standards. Once, when I ordered an old fashioned, the bartender recognised me and asked if he could take a picture of me with the drink he had made me so he could post it on Instagram for *his* credibility—he had passed the Steve Sims test of making an old fashioned, and he knew that was a big deal.

My eldest son, who was so embarrassed to table bounce, will now go into a bar and send a drink back: "I'm sorry. There's something wrong with this. Could you make me another one?" He's always very polite, but his standards mean that he won't accept a substandard drink. (Of course, when he started doing this, I laughed.)

Standards don't have to be costly, but they do have to be definitive.

SETTLING AND YOUR BANK ACCOUNT

There are going to be many times in your life when you're ruled by your bank balance—when you want to purchase something but can't afford it.

Years ago, I was renting a house that had a Viking grill on the patio. It was incredible. This home's outdoor dining centre was beautiful, and I was in love with the entire setup, but the barbecue unit was the cherry on top. I loved it so much, I looked up how much it cost: seven grand.

My first thought was, *Jeepers, I'm not buying that. It's way too expensive, but it really is brilliant*. However, I live in California, which means we spend about 60 per cent of our year cooking outside. I wasn't in the UK anymore, where you have to wait for the two days of sunshine a year.

When we moved to a new house, another rental, it didn't come with an outdoor barbecue unit. I was heartbroken. I went to a Viking dealership and salivated over the barbecue units. I could even tell the salesman more about the unit than he could because I was so obsessed with them (and did my research).

All entrepreneurs do that, don't we? We say, "That watch is the watch I want because..." and we've got all the top ten reasons. We become obsessed with whatever it is we want. That was me with this Viking grill. However, I was in a period of growth, so money had to go elsewhere. I didn't have the liquidity that I needed to get it. I thought to myself, *Well, we're going to be eating outside, so I still need to get something.*

I ended up buying myself a Weber grill that came with charcoal and a starter kit. With this one, you had to get the coals up to temperature before you could cook, which took time. Then you had to shift the coals to the right place, which got ash everywhere. There was no control, no cleanliness, and no instant on and off. You couldn't run outside, flip a switch, slap a hamburger on there, turn it off, and come back inside. Instead, there was a complicated, dirty, time-sucking process you had to follow.

It was, though, cheaper than the Viking unit. But, after a few weeks, I realised that it wasn't cooking enough food at one time, so I had to go back and buy a bigger one. I did, which meant I also needed to buy more coal—and it still wasn't clean, fast, or easy to use.

In the end, I calculated that the Viking I eventually bought only cost me $1,500 more than the money I spent on the *two* Weber grills and all the extras they needed. I was following a false economy. Today, whenever I'm looking at something to buy—and this is a typical go-for-stupid mentality—I ask myself, *What do I really want?* If I want a TV, do I want a 60-inch, 85-inch, or a 105-inch?

Consider what you want, rather than what you can afford.

Some of you are saying to yourself, *That's great, but you have to be sensible.* You're absolutely right: you do have to be sensible. You have to know when to control your impulses. That's the beauty of this exercise.

Knowing what you want doesn't mean you have to be reckless. There's a difference between *going* for stupid and *being* stupid. In fact, there's a massive difference.

Consider the TV example. You want the 105-inch, but all you can afford at the moment is the 85-inch. First, ask yourself if you have a TV at the moment. Can you wait six months to upgrade? After all, technology improves so quickly that the 105-inch will be the same price in six months as the 85-inch is right now. Never settle, but know there is a time you have to consider your options. Decide if what you are buying is going to be a false economy because you're just going to sell it in six months, or if that 85-inch will work very well for you and last you five or more years, at which time you can then upgrade your standards.

Too often, people dictate their want list by first deciding what they can afford. "I want a TV. What can I afford? Now, what's available at that price." This is the wrong way to choose what you want. Look at what you want—what meets your standards—and then look down.

A long time ago, Tony Robbins said, "You got an 'I want' list and an 'I need' list." The 'I needs' are paying your phone bill and mortgage and school fees and healthcare. You always find a way to get what you need. You rarely get what you want.

Instead of having two separate lists, I have them combined. On my phone, I keep a note that includes:

- New roof
- Kids' school fees
- Dog surgery for back leg
- New premier motorcycle
- Fly to Tokyo

My wants are integrated within my needs. It's essential to combine the two. It's true most people will get what they need but seldom what they want, but if they make what they want a need, they will work to get that exact want, rather than fit the want to their financial restrictions.

No one reading this book is working nine to five, thinking, *This is it for the rest of my life*. You're aggravated because you want more. The solution is to commit to your standards and work hard enough to have your income be able to support it. Doing it the opposite way around has never worked out for anyone.

GO FOR STUPID

Ask yourself these three questions and answer them in the space below.

1. What did you buy because you could afford it and regretted it?

....

2. What are the three things you need right now?

....

3. What are the three things you want?

....

CHAPTER SEVEN

DO YOU HAVE A KENNETH?

One of my speakeasy events was held in San Francisco, and while it was a very cool event, the point of this story is about a bartender.

Everyone who attended the event stayed at the Virgin Hotel. I had a speaking gig the day before the event was due to start, so I arrived early and decided to have lunch at the hotel restaurant. The bar in this place was impressive, stocked with all kinds of eclectic alcohol, including several Japanese whiskeys, many of which were half-full—meaning they were used and used often.

The waiter came over for my order and asked if I wanted to have a cocktail with my meal. As you just learned about me in the previous chapter, I have very high standards when it comes to my cocktails. I said, "How good is your old fashioned?" The waiter looked at me funny—he probably thought he was dealing with a prima donna—but he assured me the bartender was good.

"Okay," I said. "Just make sure it's good."

I must have intimidated him a bit because he walked over to the bartender, spoke to him for a moment, and then the bartender pranced over to me like he was Bambi on steroids.

"You asked if I can do a good old fashioned?" he said.

"Yeah, that's all I asked."

"How do you like it?"

I've always had a problem with that question. Every bartender has their own tweak on it, for starters, and if I have to essentially make it myself, it takes a bit of the fun out of it. But I went ahead and explained, "I like a decent bourbon, and I like a large ice cube. But mainly, I just want to make sure it's good. If you're proud of your old fashioned, if you would drink your own old fashioned, that's the one I want you to make."

He nodded and said, "Okay. I'm not going to give you what you asked for, but I'll be back."

He skipped back to the bar, and a few minutes later, the waiter came back with a drink and a napkin listing the ingredients. The drink he made wasn't technically an old fashioned, but he took a risk to give me something unique. And let me tell you, this was an absolutely brilliant drink.

It was so good I took a picture of it next to the napkin, a stealthy picture of the bartender, whose name was Kenneth, behind the bar, and posted them to Facebook page, saying,

"Very rarely do I get wowed by an old fashioned, but my boy Kenneth blew me away." I finished my drink, ate my lunch, and went to my speaking gig.

Over the afternoon and evening, the sixty attendees of my speakeasy appeared, and all of the ones who stopped by the bar asked for Kenneth to make them a Sims Old Fashioned. So many of them asked for it, in fact, that the hotel had to go out and get more of the Yamazaki 12 he used (which is a Japanese whiskey).

The next night the group decided to meet in the bar before going to a party that I had put together for the attendees. As I walked into the restaurant, Kenneth came sprinting at me and threw himself onto me, arms around my neck and legs around my waist, crying. After he calmed down and removed himself from me, he said, "I have never been so wanted. I had no idea who you were." People had shown him the post, and he looked me up. He was over the moon. He asked for some pictures with me and even brought his friends into the bar to meet me.

IS IT THE HOTEL OR THE PERSON?

The next day I was at the rooftop bar with one of my friends, Nic, who had come to the speakeasy with me. As we were chatting, I told him how much I loved the hotel. Nic looked at me like I was crazy.

"Are you kidding?"

I said, "No. This is brilliant. I absolutely love it."

He was shocked. His impression of the hotel was horrible. I couldn't believe we had such different opinions about the hotel that we were staying at. I told him my Kenneth story, and a light went on in his mind.

"Order a drink, right now," he told me.

Strange request, I thought, but I followed his instructions—or I tried to. I basically had to lasso one of the staff to come and serve me what was a mediocre, over-iced, horrible thing in a glass. I realised what Nic had already figured out. My entire view of the Virgin Hotel had been painted by Kenneth.

I fell in love with the entire hotel, the entire experience, because of the way that Kenneth treated me. Nic didn't meet Kenneth, so Nic met these little, tiny servers that really weren't paying attention. When you analysed the entire visit, Nic was right. It was a terrible hotel, apart from Kenneth.

A few months later, a group of us were in the area, so we stopped by to see Kenneth. But he wasn't there. We tracked him down and showed up at the new bar he was working at. Kenneth made such an impression on me that not only did I do a podcast episode about him, I went through the trouble of tracking him down when I was in town so I could get another fantastic drink from him.

My question to you is: does your business have a Kenneth?

Kenneth wasn't just a bartender; he was a mixologist. He's an artist, without a doubt. While I never got the traditional drink I ordered from him, it was because he always went and made something better. He went out of his way to give me something that would wow me, that would impress me. He took it on himself to make my experience as great as he could, even before he knew who I was.

Who, at your business, is going above and beyond to ensure that your clients are impressed? Who is making sure they are wowed every time they interact with your company? We all know that marketing, promotion, branding, and all of that other stuff is important, but when it comes down to it, the first interaction you have with someone under your brand is what sets the pace for your company, your product, your service.

I challenge you to look at your team very aggressively. Go through your roster and ask yourself, *Which one of these is a Kenneth? If I was out ill, who could stand up, hold the fort, express my tone, express my passion, and express what I stand for?* The sad truth is once you start examining your list, you'll find a bunch of people who are only working for the pay cheque. You may want to get rid of some of those people.

If you look through your whole list and can't find a single Kenneth, it's time to find yourself one.

WHO'S ON YOUR FRONT DOOR?

It's no secret that I love motorcycles. I love going for a ride on the weekend with my sons or wife. I'm always on the lookout for the next best bike.

I buy my motorcycles based on how I'm treated as I walk into the dealership. There are great motorcycles out there that I won't touch because of the treatment I received at that dealership. Your business may not have a salesperson greeting your clients as they walk in the door, but you probably have a receptionist. When a receptionist treats you with arrogance or they're ignorant, you don't want to go back to that business again.

One of my sons was recently shopping for some chinos, and I told him where he could go online to get great chinos on sale. He insisted we had to go to a specific store, so we hopped on our bikes (imagine me, hopping) and drove thirty minutes out of our way to go to this store that he liked, all so he could try on multiple pairs of chinos from different brands. In the end, he decided to purchase the brand I had recommended hours ago—and that was cheaper online. However, he didn't care about the price. He loves buying clothes from this particular store because he enjoys the experience they provide.

If a prospective customer's final decision ever comes down to focusing on the price tag of your product or service, it's because you failed to demonstrate the value or create an experience for them. Creating an experience is key to a successful business, no matter what the market is doing.

I have always focused on providing such an incredible experience for my customers that they are going to focus on that over the price tag. Why? Because they know they can't get this experience anywhere else.

There's always going to be a depression or recession or adjustment or inflation or downturn—whatever you want to call it—looming in the future. And this scares a lot of entrepreneurs and business owners. However, if you have a valuable product, if you have something that can answer a customer's problem, a recession or depression is going to help you. The only thing that happens in a downturn is customers focusing on where they are spending their dollars. They know that where their money goes has to count.

Adversity is a great benefactor to a valuable product. If it's just a shiny new thing that doesn't actually help with a problem or add value to their life, no one is going to buy it. But if it's valuable? People will stop spending money on the less valuable junk and purchase your offering instead. When the economy is really, really good, it's really, really bad for competition.

Rough seas make great sailors. And good entrepreneurs make a lot of money during adversity periods.

GO FOR STUPID

1. Who is the first person a prospect meets when introduced to your company/brand?

   ....

2. Your chain is only as strong as your weakest link. Do you have a weak link on your front line?

   ....

3. Do you have a Kenneth in your company? What's their name?

   ....

CHAPTER EIGHT

DON'T SELL THE ITEM, SELL THE REACTION

In 2018, I hosted a speakeasy in Reno.

Speakeasies are my version of a reverse mastermind. We've all been to events that are being held at a convention centre for a certain number of days, with a long line-up of speakers. The host company gives you enough information up front for you to conclude whether or not it's the kind of event you want to attend.

That's a great method, to be sure. But, in typical entrepreneur fashion, I wondered if it could be done a different way. I decided my speakeasy should focus on a topic and not the actual speakers. When I started producing my speakeasies, I challenged myself to host them in quirky locations—and not give any advance warning where we were going.

The locations are never repeated, but to hold any event in

Reno is questionable from the start. But I had a good reason—I just didn't tell the attendees. When I sold the tickets (at $2,000 a pop), I said, "You'll meet me here at 8:30 in the morning, promptly, and I'll bring you back at 5:00 p.m." That was the entirety of what they knew when they signed up.

In the morning, after everyone was loaded onto the bus, I took my group to the newest industry on the planet: Elon Musk's Gigafactory (which happens to be located in Reno). I had set up a private tour of the facility, which is housed in the second largest building that currently exists in the world. (The largest building in the world? The one Elon is currently building in China.) To give you an idea of its magnitude, it would take eight minutes to drive around the outside of the building in a Tesla. It is gigantic.

The coolest feature of the Gigafactory is that it was built with the ability to have the walls removed. It was built as a modular construction building so whenever a section needs to be expanded, the outside wall can be removed, the footings and roof extended, and the wall put back on. It's like playing with Legos, but on a much larger scale.

Tours of the Gigafactory are rarely allowed, so my group had a unique chance to see what very few people besides the workers were allowed to see. The guide took us through most of the building; we were able to see work done on solar roof panels, new battery technology, and Tesla cars. We weren't allowed to take photos (for obvious reasons), but we were able to see first-hand how Elon runs a factory—it was phenomenal.

After the factory tour, we came outside, where Elon had

loaned out a fleet of Teslas for my group to test drive. And because he owned thousands of acres all around the factory, we were able to drive wildly fast around what was basically our own racetrack circulating the Gigafactory.

Driving like we were after the Borg-Warner Trophy worked up an appetite, and thankfully, the guides at Gigafactory thought ahead. By the time we finished our test drives, they had several taco trucks lined up so we could get our energy back for the next part of the day.

I ordered everyone back on the bus, and we took off for part two of our school trip. (A school trip vibe was what I had decided to put together. No one was expecting this or knew what was going on.)

I took them from the newest profession in the world to the oldest.

Thirty minutes after loading onto the bus, we arrived at the Moonlite BunnyRanch brothel. Included in my group was a current court judge and several lawyers. About 60 per cent of the attendees were female. And I had decided to take them all to a brothel.

On the trip over, everyone was joking and chatting, "Where are we going now? What could top the Gigafactory?" As we pulled through the gates and up the drive to the violently pink building that is BunnyRanch, the entire bus went completely quiet. You could have heard a pin drop.

A friend of mine leaned forward, touched me on the arm, and

said, "I know you like to do risky things, but this is either going to go really well or really south—fast. Let's see." And then he leaned back in his chair. I thought, *How is this going to go?*

The bus slowed to a halt, the doors slid open, and I jumped out to greet Air Force Amy and Alice Little (two very famous BunnyRanch prostitutes). They were dressed for work, with their breasts about to fall out of their curve-hugging dresses at one o'clock in the afternoon.

We had travelled from the height of technology to a house of ill repute—and no one knew how to react.

Slowly, intimidatingly, the group started to exit the bus. I turned to them and asked, "Should we get a group picture in front of the brothel?" There were definitely some people that immediately and firmly stated, "I am not going to be in any photographs of this event." Sure, no problem. The rest of the group agreed, and we got a great picture.

Once inside, Amy and Alice gave us a tour of the ranch. As we went into the rooms, we saw different contraptions, chairs, and cupboards full of toys—and because many of the attendees were entrepreneurs, curiosity started to eat away at them. Before long, they were opening up drawers, poking around, and asking what every item was for. The women happily explained, in detail, what each item did.

Soon enough, they were asking to get pictures of themselves sitting in the chairs or by the cupboards, and each time the women said, "Absolutely."

I'm very proud to say that about 98 per cent of the group—there were a few that weren't happy with the event—still talk about the time they visited BunnyRanch and how fantastic a time they had.

And the best part is, it got better.

WHAT DO YOU REALLY SELL?

The point of this speakeasy was to challenge the group to see how other people's lives and professions were—both in the technology and sex industries—and to think differently in different locations. As we walked around the ranch, they were able to interact with both patrons and professionals. At the end of the tour, they took us to a large area where we could have a conversation.

Three of the women sat in a line at the front of the room and talked to us about all kinds of topics.

One of the women told us how they knew if a potential client had money. We all had a chuckle when she said, "Let's be honest. When guys come to a brothel, they never wear a watch. They leave it at home or locked in their glovebox because, for some reason, all guys think prostitutes steal your watch. We don't want your watch."

She kept going, "But because they never wear a watch, you can't use it to figure out if the guy has any money. At this point, he hasn't taken his wallet out yet either, so you can't look at it to see if it's tattered or worn down."

The women at BunnyRanch need to be able to look at a potential client and know if he has the money to get the services he wants before he gets them. So, how can you recognise if your target market has the ability to pay for what it wants? This skill is essential, whether you're selling sex, cars, jewellery, software, or coaching services. Every business owner or worker needs to make sure that, first, the potential client has the desire to make a purchase, but more importantly, they have the means to cover it.

They explained they have a trick. "Before they can book a room, we take them over to the bar,"—which is located in the front lobby of the ranch—"sit them down, and have a drink and chat with them. The chairs at the bar are higher than the average chair, so the first thing every guy does is pick up his foot to put it on the bottom rung of the barstool. When he does, we look at his socks."

I piped up, "Yeah, hang on a minute. You do what?" The ladies chuckled at my incredulity.

"We always check out a guy's socks. Men can pretend to have money, and they might turn up in a nice suit. But very few poor men focus on their underwear or socks. We always know if we're onto a good client if they've got decent socks."

We were dumbfounded, and then someone asked what other warning signs they noticed.

"A guy who shows up with a black belt and brown shoes or vice versa. If he's not paying attention to that detail, what other details is he ignoring? He doesn't have to be in a suit for us to take him seriously. He could be in jeans and a t-shirt, but if he has standards, he won't let himself down on good underwear and good socks."

This was quite enlightening to the attendees—and to me as well.

But one of the most surprising facts was about how little sex some of their clients have: "I've had the same client for eight months. He comes in once a week, but I've only had sex with him three times."

After some quick mental math, I had the thought, *Well, he's lost out.* I was confused until she explained to us that while most people think that men go to brothels for sex, in reality, they go for connection.

Today, men are terrified to walk up to a woman at the bar and get rejected and accused of being sleazy, out for sex, or objectifying women. Let's be real: guys are not great at meeting new people to begin with. There is nothing more embarrassing than being a young man trying to chat up a girl he's terrified of. Most men today are physically terrified of communication.

The women told us that many men come to BunnyRanch to rent a room, order a pizza, watch the game, tell jokes and chat with the girls, and then go home. That's it. No physical interaction at all.

Everyone was caught off guard. They taught us about communication and how necessary it is to people—and more importantly, how bad and scared we are of it today.

One of the attendees was a trainer for some of the biggest jewellery firms on the planet and had even trained staff for Tiffany. She started getting into the conversation, asking, "So how do you actually connect with people?" At this point, I thought it would be a great idea to have her go sit up front with the three prostitutes to have this conversation about communication.

The trainer continued on and also asked the prostitutes, "And what about the sex? Aren't you selling sex, and doesn't that mean it's a little bit fraudulent that they're not getting sex?"

One of the women said, "Oh yeah, they always think prostitutes are going to be absolutely amazing. You know, 'Hey, they're professionals. They have to know some tricks that my local girlfriend doesn't.' The truth is it can only go in a certain few places." That definitely earned her a laugh. "But, really, we're not selling sex. We're selling connection and intimacy. Intimacy can be a cuddle, or it can be a conversation. So what we're really selling is conversation."

She turned to the trainer and asked, "What do you sell?"

"I train people in jewellery."

"So you are selling jewellery."

"Well, no."

The woman grinned, "What do you mean?"

"We sell the emotion. Actually, what we really sell is the reaction."

Everyone clamoured for her to explain. "While I was working at Tiffany, people would tell me, 'You sell engagement rings.' I always responded, 'No. We've never sold an engagement ring in the history of the company.' I'd get a funny look, and they'd say, 'But that's what you have in your jewellery store.' That's the wrong way to think of it.

"When you come into Tiffany's looking for an engagement ring, you're looking for something to use during an incredibly important moment of your life—a moment that will be whispered and talked about with passion for decades to come. *That's* what we're selling."

She continued to explain the purchase process to us: "When you're looking at the rings and find one you want to see closer, I trained employees to pull the ring out, put it in a ring presentation box, and then bring the box to the customer. But we don't just place that box on the counter. Instead, we hold the box out to the client and say, 'Okay, what would their reaction be when they see this?' And then we open up the box. We're putting the customer in the moment when their partner sees that ring. Now they're seeing the reaction. The price: that's just the fuel you have to stick in the car. If you want this reaction, you have to pay this price. Screw the ring: is the reaction worth it?"

Everyone was amazed, but the prostitutes were nodding along. They were selling connection; they were selling permission. You can't walk up to a girl in a bar and go, "Hey, I've got a funny joke. You want me to tell you?" because nine times out of ten, they're not going to want to talk to you. But you can pay for a positive reaction when you book a room at BunnyRanch, which gives you the ability to tell jokes to a girl without fear of judgment.

You don't sell the item; you sell to the reaction. In my concierge days, I was never selling access to dinner at the feet of *David*, I was never selling the trip to go and see the Titanic, and I was never selling the backstage passes to meet Taylor Swift.

I was providing my clients with the ability to tell a cocktail story. I was creating a memory. I was giving them a positive association the next time they heard that person's voice or saw that film. I was selling an experience, an emotion, a reaction, and an association—never the event or item.

If you sell the item, that's a transaction. If you're selling a transaction, that's what Amazon does. (We'll talk more about this in the next chapter.) You may not realise it yet, but when you're only selling transactions, Amazon's already replicating what you do.

DARE TO DO THINGS DIFFERENTLY

When the goal is to sell the reaction, you have to be willing to work and think differently. If everyone else is sending out emails, then send out a letter. If everyone is making phone calls, send out an email.

You have to look at what everyone else on the planet is doing and then go for stupid and do it differently. You want your client to be shocked by the fact that you do things differently because people like creativity. Whenever I work with clients, I always stay away from the status quo.

For example, say I wanted to have a meeting with a potential client, and I knew they were into cars. I would find a car magazine, rip the centre pages out, and send it to them with a note that said, "Hey, I'd love to have a coffee with you to chat about a few things. If you agree to the coffee meeting, I'll give you the missing pages."

The people I am trying to land are millionaires and billionaires. They can afford the magazine. In fact, they probably already have the magazine—along with every single car mentioned in it.

The missing pages weren't why they agreed to the meeting every time. It was the fact that I showed them that I think and work differently than everyone else trying to land a meeting with them.

I started doing things differently decades ago. I've always gone for stupid, so I've always been willing to dare to try something new, with no guarantee it was going to work.

There's an old saying, "Every time you do anything, it'll be shit...until you've been doing it for a while." The first time I recorded a podcast, I was terrible. The first time I planned a trip, it went terribly. Get going, then get good.

Often, I'll try an idea out small first, and if it gets a good response, I'll put more effort and energy into it. If it's a complete failure, I'll ask myself, "Where did I fail, and what can I learn for my next stupid idea?"

Here's another real-life example for you. A few years ago, we were moving to a new home, and while we were packing up the cupboards, I found a box of old Christmas cards. My wife asked, "What are we going to do with these cards? We should just throw them away." It was the middle of June, and they were extremely cheap, ugly Christmas cards, but I said, "No way. I have to be able to use them somehow."

"We're not saving them for seven months for you to send out lousy cards."

"You're right. Let's send them out now."

My wife gave me *the* look. "You're going to send out Christmas cards...in June?"

"Yeah, let's try it."

For this first try, I wrote a short message in each card that went something like this:

Hey, Joe!

I know how busy it gets at Christmas, and I wanted to be the first one to send you a card. That's how important you are to me.

All the best,

Steve

I sent them out two days later. After all, you never actually send out Christmas cards on Christmas, do you? They arrive late November through early January. I had just sent out my cards in June.

I expected a few people to call me up and say, "You're a moron." But the response was far better than I could have ever expected.

Most of the people took photographs of the terrible cards and posed them on social media with captions along the lines of, "A guy I know just sent me a Christmas card in June. This guy thinks differently."

They were doing my marketing *for me*. I had people reaching out asking why they didn't get a Christmas card. (I only had thirty.) My ROI was remarkable: at least 80 per cent of the recipients responded. The result was incredible—because no one else had ever done something like this before.

Of course, my next thought was, *I can't do this again*. Why? Because: A) I had already done it once, and B) everyone had already told their friends about it. I needed to do something at least slightly different to showcase my creativity.

The following year, I decided to use a QR code (they were new and trendy at the time). If you've never used a QR code, they're simple: you hold your phone over what is essentially a square barcode, it pops up a link to a website page, and when you click the link, the link opens on your phone's browser.

I recorded a video, posted it on a secret page on my website, and generated a QR code that pointed to that URL. Then, I printed off the QR code and put it in the new batch of Christmas cards. All of this is easy enough for anyone to do. Again—because there is nothing funnier than a really lousy, stupid, non-funny Christmas card—I purchased several packs of fifty cards for $15 each from Amazon. I was able to buy the already cheap cards at a discount because no one is buying Christmas cards in the middle of summer.

The QR codes were scotch-taped onto the left side of the card—it couldn't look cheaper or rougher than that!—and wrote a message: *Hey! I wanted to be the first person to send you a Christmas card. Take a picture of this QR code.* And I drew a little arrow to it.

The best part of this was that I had my kids tape and write for me, so I didn't even have to do it myself. They did it, begrudgingly, with very strong opinions on the idea: "You're a moron, Dad. No one is going to pay attention to this."

The video was short and sweet. In it, I said, "Hey, I'm glad you got the card. I just wanted you to know that you are important to me. I know that, come Christmas, everyone's going to send you a card. You're going to get Christmas cards from your insurance agent and your gardener and your milkman—and you don't even get milk! You're going to get all of these cards, shove them up on your shelf, and then throw them away on Boxing Day. I didn't want to be lost in the crowd, so you've got a card, and you've got a video early, telling you you're special. Have a great Christmas."

I sent these cards out to over two hundred people, and again, they did the exact same thing: "My coach [or my mentor, my trainer, my favourite author] sent me this card today!"

Once again, they handled my own promotion for me. In fact, it went so well that I can't actually do it too often. Several of my coaching clients have taken and run with this same idea, and I advise them not to do it every year or else people will come to expect them, and it will lose its magic. The key is to be sporadic. One year, send an early Christmas card. Two years later, send out an Easter or Halloween card.

One year, on the first of January, I sent several clients a birthday card. Inside it said, *I know I always miss your birthday, so this year, I wanted to be the very first person to wish you a happy birthday.*

Dare to be different.

You can't stand out until you're willing to stand up. Too many people try to stand up by conforming to what everyone else is doing. That way leads to a poppy field: everyone looks exactly the same.

Today, everyone claims to be different...by telling you how unique they are on a website that looks like every other company's. Be a unicorn and be prepared to disrupt the status quo, whether you are creating an advertising campaign, writing copy, shooting videos, or running a sequence.

IT'S NOT ABOUT THE MONEY

Most entrepreneurs have a fear that in order for them to do something different, they have to shell out a lot of capital. However, there's a difference between cost and care. Don't look at the price tag—look for the impact, even if it only costs $2.

Years ago, I attended a party that was hosted by a client from my concierge days. He had private jets (plural), exotic cars, and was a massive wine connoisseur. There were easily three hundred people invited to his birthday party. He enjoyed being the centre of attention, so he planned to uncork several expensive, special wines during the party.

Standing in line outside the house, I met a pair of young men in front of me who ran a jet charter company and had attended in the hopes of doing business with the host. While we waited, they turned around and (tried) to make small talk. Eventually, they asked me, "What did you bring him for his birthday?"

"Oh, I just got him a little thing. What did you get him?"

They held up a bag housing six bottles of wine. "We know he likes wine, so we got him these."

"I didn't know you two knew anything about wine."

"Well, we don't really. But we did some research."

I stared at them in astonishment. "Let me get this straight. You're turning up to a billionaire's party, who you know is a wine aficionado, with six bottles of wine in a bag because the counter clerk at BevMo told you they were great. That's what you're stepping into this room with?"

They were mortified when they realised what they had done. They knew they couldn't compete with the host on wine knowledge, so they had tried to compete on price tag. However, to them, $50–100 was an expensive bottle of wine. The host had spent over $10,000 on a single bottle of wine.

Here they were, turning up with six bottles of okay wine, trying to look as though they had paid attention to what he liked. Instead, they had demonstrated they hadn't.

I tried to calm them down. "Don't worry, boys. He'll never know these came from you."

"What do you mean?"

I gestured around us. "Look at how many people are here. He's not going to be standing at the door, welcoming these gifts. No one's going to know who gave him what."

They didn't believe me. "No, no, no, no, you're wrong," they scoff. "He'll be up there, and when we give him this wine, we'll make a joke of it."

"Fair enough," I said. "I don't want to be there for that."

But, as we made it through the front door, gave our names, and showed our IDs, an assistant took the bag of wine from them and shoved it onto a table that was overflowing with other boxes and bags of gifts. The guys stared, and I had to give them a gentle nudge to get them moving into the party proper.

"All right, there you go. You're safe," I told them. "Trust me, you dodged a bullet. Don't worry about it." And we went our separate ways.

Everyone who has been with me at a party will tell you I am not a good party person. I made a beeline for the end of the bar, ordered my old fashioned, and sat down to people-watch (reminiscent of my doorman days). Within a few minutes, the two young men wandered back over to me and started chatting me up because they had found out what I did and wanted me to convince my clients to use their jet services.

Finally, I had to be blunt. "Boys, look. If it comes up, I'll mention your business. But I'm not really interested, and I'm not interested in talking about it, especially right now."

As I was letting them down, the host himself bounded over and started chatting to me. He glanced down at my old fashioned and mock shuddered, "You're not drinking any wine?"

I laughed, "I don't know shit about wine. The last thing I'm going to do is ask the bartender for a glass of wine when I don't know what I'd be ordering. I'd be way out of my depth. I like my old fashioned, and I'm sticking to it." That got a booming laugh out of him.

Then I said, "However, my wife loves wine, and she always makes me uncork it for her. The worst part is how many times I've sliced my fingers up on that blasted foil on the top of the wine. Does that ever bother you?"

He was already nodding. "Yeah, it does. And there's all that wax you have to pop off."

"Yes! It always seals the top and is annoying to try and peel off. I complained so much my wife got me a foil cap remover. You literally clamp it onto the top, spin it, and it cuts into the foil. When you pull it off, it takes off the foil *and* the wax in one go. I haven't cut my fingers since."

"That sounds great! I'll have to look into it."

I reached into my pocket and pulled out a tiny inch-by-two-inch box that was wrapped in happy birthday wrapping paper. I held it out to him and said, "I got one for you. Happy birthday, mate. You'll never cut your fingers again."

He took it, unwrapped it right there, opened it up, and said, "This is great. Thank you very much."

The two guys were standing awkwardly off to the side, watching the encounter, and slowly sinking into a puddle of embarrassment.

I had given my client a way of enjoying what he loved *more*, and I did it not by competing with a price tag but by competing with care. I gave him a relatable solution to a problem that everyone has—that horrible foil on the top of a bottle of wine.

Later that night, he called court to do his wine unveiling: "I have these cases full of wine, and we're going to uncork them together. They're all from an exceptional vintage, and everyone is going to get a glass."

He pulled a bottle out, shoved his hand into his back pocket, and pulled out the foil remover I had given him just a few hours earlier. Within seconds, he had removed the wax and foil. It would have made the perfect QVC advertisement, it worked so well.

As it came off, he yelled, "Big shout out to Sims! Best gift on the planet." I was still in the back at the bar with my old fashioned. I held it up and yelled back, "Cheers!"

Most people pay attention to the price tag of a gift rather than the purpose.

Another client of mine collected shoes. Yeah, shoes. He would buy leather from every place he travelled (Africa, Venice, Paris, Asia) and send it to a gentleman in Paris who would make him custom shoes.

I knew there was absolutely no way I could compete with these custom-made, extraordinarily expensive shoes. However, I also knew that after 9/11, you couldn't get on a plane with a metal object in any shape or form.

As a present to celebrate a successful event, I sent him a shoehorn made out of bone. I included a note that said, *I know you like to kick your shoes off when you travel, but when you have to put them back on, you don't want to risk ruining the rear support. Since you can't take your metal shoehorn on the plane anymore, here's one out of bone.*

What he didn't know was that I had gotten a pack of two off Amazon for $12. For $6, I had given him a present that he loved and used every single time he travelled.

Don't focus on only trying to give presents that are the exact item someone loves. Give them something that will assist or amplify the pleasure they'll receive from that item they love. Dare to think differently, even about something as small as a gift.

Good gifts, like a well-thought product or service, are about the reaction, the feeling, the memory—not the object itself or the dollar amount.

GO FOR STUPID

Ask yourself these three questions and answer them in the space below.

1. How can you reframe what you do by looking at the reaction rather than the transaction?

....

2. What is the cheapest item you can purchase that would aid or amplify a hobby or interest of your client/prospect?

....

3. What is the cheapest gift you've ever given someone that has produced the biggest smiles?

....

CHAPTER NINE

AMAZONIFICATION

One of the most common experiences during the pandemic that's being discussed as we reminisce in our post-COVID days is how the situation amplified the good or bad in your life and business. It's like drinking alcohol: if you are in a happy mood and you have a couple of sips, you get happier and giggly, but if you are depressed and you sink a couple of shots, your mental state will continue to deteriorate. The alcohol itself doesn't change how you feel; it amplifies your current mood.

At the start of COVID, if we had a bad relationship within our home, being forced to live with each other twenty-four hours a day amplified the stress we were already experiencing. On the professional side, if we had a business that was thriving online, COVID amplified the rewards and even provided new opportunities.

However, if our business was unstable—even unknowingly—COVID amplified how bad it was. In fact, I lost a business during COVID.

Before the pandemic, I didn't realise how weak the company was. COVID magnified the flaws in the business. I'm grateful for the clarity because it saved me at least ten years of trying to make a business work that was doomed to fail from the start.

The company (which will remain nameless) was a wide-catch business that diluted the exclusive brands we had worked with in the past into a mass market version of a travel company. COVID showed me the copious number of holes we had in our marketing reach. There were so many areas the company would have to compete in that we would have had to work at least three times as hard to stand out in an industry where there was a margin compression of attention.

Today, if you want to purchase a pair of shoes, there are hundreds, if not thousands, of websites you can look at. Yet I'm amazed at how many people look up shoes on Nike's website, then complete the purchase on Amazon.

The same thing was happening to us. While there were a lot of websites out there, there was a compression of attention, meaning that customers might look up options on our website but would complete the purchase somewhere else. We were spending piles of money to market and brand ourselves as the optimum choice for purchase.

As our costs increased, our margins decreased until our profit margins weren't there. If COVID hadn't happened, we would have continued to carry on as we were, spending money hand over fist. But because everyone was at home—and most people were focusing on online shopping for the first time ever—online businesses such as Instacart, Dominoes, and Amazon blew up. Society's new shopping habits were working out great for them, but they weren't working out so well for my company.

Once I realised what was happening, I spoke to my partners. "Look, these are the problems we're facing—and they aren't going to go away. In fact, they're going to continue to be amplified. What are we going to do?"

We all agreed it was smarter to shut the company down after eighteen months rather than continuing to pour money into it just to find that we have the same exact problems ten years down the road. We looked at this decision in a positive light because it allowed us to focus on other elements of our other businesses—such as Sims.Media.

THE GOOD AND BAD OF AI COMMUNICATION

Sims.Media is a media company I created in partnership with my son. We analyse how industries form habits and how customers respond and react to those habits—and vice versa, such as viewing items on Nike but purchasing on Amazon. By deep diving into these habits, we are able to create media campaigns that work with those habits in dozens of different industries.

One of the habits we noticed growing was in the world of AI (artificial intelligence). People joke about robots taking over the world, but the reality is they are already here, and the increase in AI is not going to slow down. We already have AI robots in our pockets, called iPhones.

The unfortunate consequence of speaking to Siri, barking orders at Alexa, and clicking buttons on Amazon, however, is that we are losing the ability to communicate properly. This, too, has been amplified by COVID: we couldn't leave the house, hang out with friends, go to the movies, or head to the pub.

When COVID hit, I was astounded by the number of people who were posting online how horrified they were that they could no longer go for a walk in the park or shopping at the mall. Any time I questioned them, "When was the last time you went for a walk or to the mall?" they would admit they hadn't been in years. (Going to the mall on a Saturday is my definition of hell.)

They were blaming COVID for their lack of ability to connect when we had really stopped connecting in 2002 with the advent of Friendster, which was quickly followed by MySpace and then Facebook. These platforms allowed us to outsource our ability to communicate by typing our celebrations into a small box.

They'd post about the birth of their new baby and then get upset if they didn't get a million likes. In 1994, when we had a new baby, we phoned up our mates, got together, and—probably inappropriately—smoked cigars and drank whiskey while looking at the infant. "Raise a dram to the new baby!"

Now we put up a banner and ask people to react with a thumbs up, thumbs down, heart, or some witty comment that is almost always taken rudely.

Our ability to communicate was not ruined by COVID—it was exposed by COVID. And to make it worse, companies latched onto it. Amazon was already taking over the online world, and after the pandemic hit, everything we wanted, we bought through them: toilet rolls, pet medicines, t-shirts, coats, a chest of drawers, beds, computers.

While I was writing this book, I purchased some Apple products for my family, and I realised that I could have them delivered the next day through Amazon, while I would have had to wait three days if I purchased through Apple. Yet when I checked on Amazon who handled fulfilment for those products, it was Apple. I'm still not sure how Apple can fulfil faster through Amazon than their own stores, but apparently they can.

I'll never know, either, because there is no one at Amazon I could ask. Both communication and purchasing today have become transactional. If you disagree with me, try to call Amazon and say, "Hey, I'm thinking of changing the toilet paper I want to buy. Which one would you suggest?" You won't get an answer because you don't have a relationship with Amazon. In fact, you can't even phone them. There is no communication because they don't want communication—they want a transaction.

LIVING IN A TRANSACTIONAL SOCIETY

We may not like it, but we have become used to a transactional society. So when someone takes the time to ask, "Why are you purchasing that particular product? What about this option?" we're surprised—borderline shocked. Imagine if you walked into Starbucks tomorrow, gave them your order, and the barista responded, "That's a great choice, but have you tried this?" Your first reaction would be aggravation.

We are in a society where you decide *I want these jeans in size 32,* click “Add to cart,” and purchase. You don’t expect a representative to stop you and say, “While those are great jeans, they have a baggier fit. Have you thought about trying this type? They have more of a slim fit, which would look great with your body type.”

You don’t expect it because no one has these conversations anymore. On top of becoming transactional, during COVID, dozens of (needed) movements happened: #MeToo, Stop Asian Hate, Black Lives Matter. The result was aggravated, violent conversations happening online. On top of *that*, cancel culture became more popular. It was a horrible cocktail where people tried to dig up something you said decades ago when you were uneducated or inebriated at a cocktail party and shame you for it now.

People love being in a gotcha society—when they are the ones getting you. The consequence of this distasteful cocktail is that everyone tries to avoid having meaningful conversations for fear of looking stupid. But we need to have these conversations. We can only become more educated and smarter when we have them, say something stupid, and allow someone else to educate us: “Have you thought about the ramifications of what you said?” or “Have you thought about how what you’re suggesting will actually work in the real world?” This opens the door for you to expand your worldview and say, “No, I hadn’t thought about that. Thank you very much.”

We run away from these conversations because of our fear of the gotcha and cancel society. Instead of learning, we say nothing. Silence has become the first line of defence.

I refuse to accept this new way of life. I would rather say something stupid and allow someone to educate me and become smarter so I don't make the same mistake again. Ignorance is never a good strategy.

Frankly, ignorance should not be tolerated. While scientists are trying to find a cure for COVID, they should also be trying to find a cure for ignorance. That would make for a much better world.

Fear of conversation has bled into our businesses. When clients come to Sims.Media, the first things they ask us are:

- How can we build up a good funnel?
- How do we build a chat bot?
- How can we build up good sequencing within the AI responses?

I stop them and explain that they can, and should, have a chat bot, but it should be staffed by human employees. Every customer can tell if they're talking to an auto-respond robot or a human being within two seconds. Providing a human chat option builds engagement. They want to respond to someone who says, "Hey, how's your day? I'm in Illinois, and I'm freezing. I hope the weather is better where you are!"

We're compelled to engage in that conversation, rather than just complete a transaction. Companies are building transactional businesses for fear of having bad communication. But there's already an organisation out there that excels in transactions: Amazon.

If you continue to build up a transactional "relationship" with your community, tribe, and clients—well, Amazon knows how to do that and can do it better than you. They're happily waiting to put you out of business.

In fact, here's some free advice for you: while you plan your transactional business so you have less overhead, spend the same amount of time updating your resume because Amazon has already put you out of business. You just don't realise it yet.

A few years ago, a company came over from the UK called Purple Bricks. Purple Bricks was an online company similar to Rocket Mortgage and Quicken Loans that enabled you to sell and buy property faster online without the necessity of an agent. Every agent on the planet said, "This ain't gonna work. Avoid Purple Bricks. You won't get to see me." And it failed. Purple Bricks failed. It closed, and it ran off the US shores with its tail between its legs.

But if you think it's over, you're wrong.

It may have lost the battle, but it didn't lose the war. You see, it gained an education in the short time it was operating in the US. I predict that we are going to see a second wave of that industry within the next few years, and it will be sharper for all the education it received from its first failure. And it will come back to a society where people are looking for ways to live from their computer screen without being challenged: "I want convenience. I don't wanna answer lots of questions. If there's a button over here I can push so I don't have to talk to someone, I'm pushing."

They're going to come back—but they won't be able to succeed *if* you challenge your clients.

CHALLENGE THE WHY

I often speak at real estate and mortgage conferences, and a few years ago, I spoke at an event in Las Vegas. After the event, I was approached by an elegant woman in her fifties, who said, "I want to be the best real estate agent in my area. I want to dominate the market. I want everyone in the area to think of me the second they think of selling or buying a property. Will you coach me?"

I was impressed by her passion and what she stood for, so I agreed to take her on. Together, we developed her brand, marketing, image, and communication methods. Everything was going great, until one day I checked my voicemail to find an out-of-breath, desperate message from her.

She had landed a career-making client, and now everything was going wrong. She explained she was putting everything I had told her into practice, but it wasn't working, and she didn't know what to do. "I just need to speak with you for a few minutes, Steve. Can you jump on a call?" I cleared some time and jumped on a video call. When the call connected, I said, "You sounded hectic. What's going on? I don't believe everything is actually terrible."

The client she had landed was a big shot in her town: an extremely successful female entrepreneur who had a lot of connections. My client wanted to look after this woman for the obvious reason that if she was successful, it could be a lead magnet for her and rocket her to a new level of clients. I fully understood why she wanted this woman as a client.

"So where's it going wrong? I know you're passionate about

your job, and I'm sure because of the pressure of helping this A-lister that you're on your game."

She was clearly frustrated with herself. "I don't know. When I connected with this woman, I asked her what she was looking for. She told me she wanted a three-bedroom house that has a swimming pool and summer house on a particular street. I dragged up everything that was available on this street, showed her, and she hated all of them. When she said no to all of those, I went a step further and started knocking on the doors of houses that were a match to what she wanted, introduced myself, and told them I had a buyer in the market and wanted to know if they were open to selling. A few people said yes, so I sent those property details to her, and again, she said no, no, no. I don't know what I'm doing wrong. The street isn't that big, and she had about 80 per cent of the street to choose from."

I didn't even have to listen to her entire explanation to know where she went wrong. I knew it within the first twenty seconds: "I know exactly where it went wrong. You didn't talk to her."

She blinked at me a few times and asked, "What do you mean?"

I told her, "You never had a conversation, and you never challenged the why. You took orders and tried to complete the transaction. 'I want a burger with fries.' 'There you go.' 'I want a side of ketchup.' 'Here it is.' The fault in this situation is yours. And there's only one way out of it."

I told her what to say when she went back to her client. "I

have to apologise. I didn't give you the service you required. You told me what you wanted, but I failed to ask one simple question, and that question is why. Why do you want a three-bedroom house? Why do you want a summer house? Why do you want a swimming pool? Why that street?"

She was nervous about going back to this A-lister and admitting she messed up. It's understandable: everyone is unnerved when they find out they're not actually in a relationship with someone and are, instead, in a transaction. Now they have to go back and begin a relationship by starting to communicate.

And she did. She said what I told her to say and challenged her client's why—which turned out to be surprising and moving.

Her client told her that when her mom was living just outside of town, any time they came into town, she would take the client to this street and tell her, "This is where I would buy a house because *this* is where the movers and shakers live. This is where the power players live. This is where the people who made it live."

Her mother passed away years ago, and now that she's the power player, she wanted to move to that street because that's what her mom always wanted. It was a trigger memory of a person she had loved and lost.

However, this street wasn't the "it" place anymore. We all know those areas of town where you wouldn't have wanted to be around once the sun went down years ago, and yet today you couldn't afford to live there because they've been gentrified. Gentrification has turned those cheap, dangerous areas into the best places to live, and the places where the trendy people lived into dumps.

Once my client realised that this woman was trying to buy a house for her mom's approval—she wanted to move to an area that would have made her mom say, "You made it, girl"—she was able to communicate more effectively. She told her client, "That's a beautiful street, but it's not *the* street. Have you ever been to this other area?"

When she had that conversation, when she dared to challenge, and when she dared to have communication with her client, she was able to sell her a home. She showed her the "it" street because she dared to start a conversation.

If you're not in a conversation, you're in a transaction. When you're in a transaction, Amazon is rewriting your job description to "unemployed."

Take a hard look at your business. Can it be replaced by Amazon? If it can, don't panic—you still have time to change the situation. All you have to do is focus on the question: "Do I have a relationship?"

If a competitor turned up tomorrow called Blue Hippo that did everything Amazon did but it was $1 cheaper, would you stay with Amazon? Of course not, because you don't have a relationship with Amazon, you have a relationship with the convenience they provide you. If a new company could do the same thing cheaper or faster, there would be a mass migration.

Don't be fooled thinking you can fake a relationship with loyalty points. "Build up points to get three cents off of the item that you didn't want in the first place!" Loyalty points are legalised bribery. No friend of mine has ever said, "Hey, come and have a drink with me. I'll give you some loyalty points." Loyalty points—or any other gimmicks—are never necessary when you have a relationship.

My challenge to you is to have the conversation, ask the stupid question, and be willing to become educated.

DARE TO ASK THE STUPID QUESTION

I was sitting in a meeting that was all about the PPR[2] return. Over and over, they mentioned PPR: "We have to make sure the PPR is correct." "Once we've analysed the PPR on this, we can forecast it."

About an hour in, I was thinking, *What the hell is a PPR?* I raised my hand and said, "Before we go to break, can you explain to me what the PPR is so I can follow this presentation?"

To my right sat two young guys with a combined age of twelve—they looked and acted like children in this meeting—who smirked and sneered at my question. I looked over at them and thought, *I don't care what they think, but they really should learn that sneering is not the smartest thing to do at a business meeting.*

The presenter looked confused. "I'm sorry?" I explained, "The

---

2 I've made up these letters. This meeting was so long ago that I don't remember the real acronym. I hope you can forgive me.

PPR. You've been referring to this PPR that you're going to analyse and forecast."

His eyes went wide. "I am so sorry. I was so nervous about giving this meeting to you all today that I misspoke. It's not the PPR. It's the PPC."[3] He had accidentally gotten the last letter wrong all morning. My question had made him realise that he was focusing so hard on the presentation that he had used the wrong abbreviation. It was a classic "Emperor's New Clothes" moment.[4]

As he explained what the abbreviation was supposed to be, the two guys to my right prayed for the floor to open and swallow them whole. Not only did they look ridiculous, they had no comeback. I leaned over to them and said, "Boys, you look stupid, but now you can become smarter. I hope that next time you risk looking stupid to ask the right question so you won't be stupid."

LOOK FOR THE SOURCE OF THE LAUGHTER

You need to understand that the person who is laughing at you is terrified.

When you're in a pub and you're going for stupid or risking looking stupid to ask a question, the guy at the end of the bar is going to laugh at you, even though he's never had a job in his life. He's laughing because he's terrified you are going to achieve what you've set out to do.

---

3 I made these letters up too.

4 "The Emperor's New Clothes" is a classic fable where someone convinces the emperor that only smart people can see his clothes, when he's really walking around naked.

When someone laughs at you, look for the source.

I went to an event recently called War Room, attended by other owners and founders of major companies. During one of the sessions, we found out that one of the attendees had just launched his company on the stock exchange. We were in the room with him on the first day of trading when his company was listed for $600 million. The presenter gave him a shout-out, and the entire room exploded with applause and cheers. We gave him a standing ovation.

At the end of the day, we jokingly told him that since he was now worth $600 million, he got to buy us all beers. He laughed and we all went out. While we were celebrating, he told me that he couldn't tell his friends about his success. When he told them he was going for a $100 million valuation launch, his friends laughed at him and told him to aim lower. (Clearly he needed to upgrade his standard of friends.) Yet having a meeting at this same conference a few years ago, one of the other founders asked him, "Hang on, why are you only going for a hundred?" He took the question to heart and went for $800 million instead. He failed, but he failed six times over his original goal. He teared up as he told me this. He was saddened by the lack of support from his friends, and he realised he needed to be in a room where people challenged him to do more.

They'll laugh at your lack of vision and your short-sightedness of what you can truly achieve—and then they'll dare you to go for stupid instead.

GO FOR STUPID

Ask yourself these three questions and answer them in the space below.

1. Do you have a relationship or a transaction with your clients?

....

2. When communicating with your customer/client, are you forming a relationship and daring to challenge their request?

....

3. What can you do to avoid creating a transaction in your sales process?

....

CHAPTER TEN

LET'S PLAY A GAME

As Sims.Media continues to grow, I've noticed a pattern in the questions that new clients ask me:

- How do I speak to this big name?
- How do I get this A-lister to see my product?
- How do I get this influencer to endorse my service?
- How can I get a picture with this celeb so that I can put it on my website?

All of these questions have a single word in common: I.

Many, many years ago, I created a game that I've used on thousands of stages, radio shows, and podcasts. It's called the Barbecue Game.

I'll choose a person to pick on, usually a man, and have him imagine this scenario: he's in my hometown, I invited him to my house this weekend for a barbecue, and he just said yes. Then I ask my victim, “What’s the first question you are going to ask me?”

Him: “What time does it start?”

Me: “Great question. Early evening, six o’clock, and it’ll go until we run out of alcohol. Second question?”

Him: “Where is it?”

Me: “Another good question. Here’s the address. What’s your third question?”

Him: “What should I wear? Is there a dress code?”

Me: “Yup, your appearance matters. It’s very casual: shorts, sandals, t-shirt. Give me a fourth question.”

Him: “Who is gonna be there?”

Me: “A mixture of celebrities, influencers, my next-door neighbour, my parents, and my mates. A wide mix of people. What’s next?”

Him: “Are cameras allowed?”

Me: “Yup, cameras allowed. Snap away and get some good memories.”

These are real answers I’ve been given when playing this game. Men usually give me between six and ten questions before they ask the right one: “Is there anything I can bring?” The ladies, however, give it to me on their first try about 99 per cent of the time. (Fun fact, the ladies have never asked me who will be there. That seems to be a purely selfish male question.)

Imagine the barbecue is a relationship. If I phone you up at eight o'clock tonight, your first thought is going to be, *How the heck did Steve get my phone number?* But that's a question for later. The second thought is going to be, *What does he want?*

And that's the point. Any time someone calls you, you know that they want something, whether it's me, your local insurance agent, your best mate, or your mom. It could be they want to tell you about something, they want to catch up on the news, find out how you are, have dinner with you, or up your insurance premium. Doesn't matter who it is; you are guaranteed that the person on the other side of that phone wants something.

This is the exact same guarantee any person you want to have a conversation with is going to have. When you approach them, they already know that you want something. You've got a stupid grin on your face as you walk up, and they know you're after something. But if you can show up to that conversation with something for the party? Now *they're* interested.

Every relationship I've ever gotten into—whether I was texting them because I found out their cell number or turning up at a party to "accidentally" bump into them—the first thing I asked myself before approaching them was "What can I bring to this party?"

Years ago, I finagled an invitation to a gala because I was trying to get a Silicon Valley VC to get into business with me. I had lightly stalked him in order to find out what kind of galas he went to and found out that he went to this specific charity event every year. I bought my ticket, did my hair, arrived at the gala, and saw him across the room with a group of friends.

I waited for a blank spot in their conversation and made my move. Now, I'm aware that I'm a big guy, and now 250-pounds of ugly was coming at him like a cruise missile. Of course, he's looking at me thinking, *This guy wants something.* He was right. I did.

Think about every celebrity who's been stopped on the street. They know you want something, and they want you to tell them what that is—but you don't. They're stuck standing there trying to figure out if you want an autograph or a photograph or something else. You walk away saying, "They're not very friendly," when the truth of the matter is *you* made them uncomfortable. Their unfriendliness is your fault.

Whenever I go up to someone I don't know, from my new neighbour to a celebrity, I do the exact same thing: walk up, stick out my hand, and say, "Hey, how're you doing? My name's Steve Sims. You don't know me." This instantly stops them from worrying and wondering who I am.

In the next breath, I tell them what I want: "I'd love to talk to you about a project you're involved in." "I'd love to talk to you about going on your podcast." "I wanna talk to you about cleaning the rubbish off of your front yard." Whatever it is I want, I get my point across, and then I quickly pivot to what I can bring to their party.

"I wanna talk to you about cleaning up your yard. My gardener is really good at doing this. Would you like me to put you in touch with them?"

"It's nice to meet you. I saw you have a nice motorcycle in your garage. I have a fantastic mechanic who specialises in motorcycles. If you've ever got a problem, I'd love to help you."

With the Silicon Valley investor, while I was researching him, I found out he was involved in a new project. When I approached him, I shook his hand and gave my spiel: "Hey, I'm Steve Sims. You don't know me. I want to chat with you about one of the projects you're involved in because I think it would be a good project for me. But first, I want to talk to you about this other project. I was chatting with my team the other day, and we came up with three things that we felt could potentially get in the way of making this a phenomenal, impactful company." These three things were what I had brought to the barbecue.

In a weird quirk of human biology, we are wired to love getting things in threes and fives instead of twos and fours. (I'm sure there's a psychologist out there who has written a whole book on why.)

When my team was coming up with our three things, we had to really stretch to find a third, but we did it so it would sound better to him. After I told him the first one, he looked at me and said, "What's the second one?" I told him, and he asked for a third, so I gave him that too.

When I was done, he started laughing. All these people around us, and this guy is looking at me and laughing. As you learned earlier in the book, happiness and laughter is contagious. He laughs, and looks at the group around us, and they start laughing at me too.

A big group of people laughing at me didn't sit too well. I thought to myself, *Well, this didn't get the response I wanted it to.* I turned to walk away, but he reached up to put his hand on my shoulder to stop me. Now he's laughing and touching me. My thought changed to, *This situation better change quickly before it gets ugly.*

I half turn back to him, and my face is looking a bit growlier than usual. He says, "No, no, no. Please don't leave. I'm sorry for laughing at you, but there's a part of the story you don't know. I killed that deal six months ago because of the second item you just told me. It's dead, and we never revive a dead deal. But what's really funny to me is that you came up with a solution for that second item that these idiots never saw."

At this point, the group around us stopped laughing. He faced me and said, "I want to work with people who dare to solve, dare to challenge, and dare to think. That deal may be dead, but would you be open to being on retainer so when I have a new deal, I can send it over and get your viewpoint on it?"

I immediately agreed, and I've been on retainer with that guy for almost a decade. Every time he sends me a deal, I get to look at it and ask stupid questions that challenge the people on the project. People hate to be asked stupid questions, but it's because they're scared. If I ask you a stupid question and you can't answer me, then who is the stupid person?

Next time you are with your family, your friends, your tribe, or your coworkers, I dare you to try the Barbecue Game on them. Try it with the men you know, and see how many questions it takes them. Then try it with the women and realise how brilliant they are.

With every single relationship you are in, ask yourself, *What can I bring to the party?*

WHO CARES WHAT YOU LOOK LIKE?

We live in a world where the visual has taken priority over credibility. It no longer matters who you are or what you've achieved. It matters to society what you look like. If you are leaning up against a fancy sports car for an Instagram post, it doesn't matter if you actually own the car or not.

I used to play a little game by myself when I was a doorman. When someone turned up at the club with an expensive watch, you always knew because they'd have their sleeve pulled up so everyone would notice it. I would make a simple comment on it to that person—"Hey, I like your watch"—and see if they took the bait. The ones who were concerned with their optics would always reply, "Oh, thanks. This was $25,000." I never asked how much it was. You would be astounded at how many people would tell me the price of the watch.

There would be some people, however, who would respond with something like, "Oh, thanks. This was my dad's watch." or "My family always loved these watches, so when I had enough money, I bought one. It makes me think of them when I look at it." There was never a mention of a price tag from those people.

The same thing happened with cars. A nice car would pull up outside the club, and the guy would put on a show getting out: standing up, looking around, and grabbing his jacket from the back seat before finally tossing his keys to the valet and saying something cliché like, "Make sure you take care of her." He moved slowly so that everyone in line for the club could see him while he pretended he didn't care if they were all staring at him or not.

Others would get out quickly and practically run to the other side so they could open the door for their partner. The car was an afterthought to taking care of the person they brought with them.

I'd give the same type of comment: "I like your car." The ones who needed to be seen would reply, "That's a limited edition, $250,000 luxury brand." And often, they'd proceed to recite a spec sheet to me.

I realised there were people who would drive the car—and for some people, the car would drive them.

I learned this lesson decades ago, but recently, I've found that's been amplified. With the rise of social media, everyone is focused on looking good or looking the part. When it comes to the world of luxury and those connected to it, you realise that they have to look and act a certain way.

I, on the other hand, never knew anything like that world, so I thought, *Why draw attention to it?* I don't look good enough to be in that world. I know I don't sound good enough to be in it. My family didn't go to Harvard or Oxford, and I didn't have any of those connections. My dad still lays bricks, and it's still raining in London.

Rather than focusing on what I looked like, I focused on addressing the problem. I put more emphasis on daring to be different and being creative than my appearance. What do you need to do to make sure that this enters your mind before entering into any relationship or conversation?

THE HEADACHE TABLET GAME

Another game I play when I'm giving talks is the headache tablet game. I tell the audience, "Let's play a little game about visual attention and its importance in your ability to make a decision." They always look a little nervous.

"It's midnight and you have a blistering headache. Who here has had a headache before?" Of course, almost everyone raises their hand. "You get out of bed, walk into the bathroom, open the medicine cabinet, and pull out your headache tablets, right?" Nods all around.

"When was the last time you looked at the box or bottle and thought, *Nah, I don't like this logo,* and then put the box back and grabbed another one?" Everyone laughs at the idea. "You see, when a product is solution-based, you don't care what it looks like."

There are two forms of marketing on the planet today: solution and aspirational.

You buy that Ferrari because you've made it. You buy that

Gucci handbag because it's what rich people use. You buy that watch because it signals you're successful. These are all examples of aspirational products. But here's the kicker: a Ferrari has a worse warranty than a Kia or Hyundai. That watch won't tell time any better than your Apple watch. That Gucci purse holds the same amount of stuff as the knockoff brand.

Most people buy to solve a problem. I'll buy that oil if it stops my wheel from squeaking. I'll buy that software to make my accounting easier. I'll buy these tablets because they make my headache go away faster. When I had my concierge business, people hired me to make their cocktail stories more interesting. (However, you have to keep your solution from becoming a commodity or Amazonified. We'll talk about that in a minute.)

Years ago, as I grew my businesses and understood there were two differentiators within marketing and branding—aspirational- and solution-based—I decided I was going to focus on solution-based ideas (because no one was aspiring to look like me). The basic difference between marketing and branding is this: branding is what people say about you when you've left the room, while marketing is what you say about you—loudly.

Over time, I realised that my brand developed because my focus was on my customer. I was forming a brand by avoiding forming one. I knew I didn't look good, so I didn't have a picture of myself on any of my profiles or my website. My brand was formed because of my resistance to brand myself.

Fast forward to today and we have a society where everyone

and every business is screaming, "Look at me! Don't you want to be exactly like me?" There are swimwear models posting a quote they found in a Hallmark Christmas card, and now they think they're a life coach.

Here's a true story that happened to me recently. I live just outside of Beverly Hills, so I often take meetings in town. Unless I have my wife or kids with me, I ride my motorcycle to my meetings, which I love but Beverly Hills hates. I had to park in the one parking tower that allows motorcycles and is about four blocks away from the heart of the city. It's annoying, but at least it lets me get my steps in.

This particular day, I parked and walked a few blocks to my meeting, which went very well. As I was walking back to my bike to go home, I noticed a bright yellow sports car in the far left-end corner of the parking tower. Two young men were leaning up against it while a third one took a video of them. The two leaning on the car were talking through a script that followed the typical influencer outline: if you want to make money, you have to follow me, sign up, buy this.

I watched them for a minute, thinking, *Oh my God, they're everywhere. There's no shame in the world. They're videoing in a car park!* What happened next had me in literal tears.

The guys were gesturing towards the camera when we heard a very angry, very large American gentleman scream at the top of his lungs, "Get the **** off my car!" Then he started sprinting through the car park towards these three guys. This guy was large enough that *I* wouldn't want to upset him, so the kids were understandably terrified. They turned tail and ran for the floor's exit as fast as their legs could carry them—but that man was hot on their trail. I wish I had been able to video this moment, but I was physically unable because I was laughing so hard that tears were obstructing my ability to see the camera button on my phone.

This was genuinely hilarious, but it's the world we live in. Wouldn't it be amazing if, in order to be called an influencer, you had to have actually achieved something first? You're an influencer in marketing because you created dozens of brilliant marketing campaigns. You're an influencer in modelling because you were a highly successful model for years.

Today, you don't have to achieve anything to influence others. Unauthorised, underachieving, unqualified people can populate their Instagram with posts of aspirational marketing to convince your eyes that this is the person you also want to be—yet just three weeks earlier, they were cleaning your carpets.

People are focused too much on what they look like. One of the biggest offenders—and the one I love speaking to the most—is the real estate industry.

IT'S NOT ABOUT YOU

How many times have you seen a flier of a young female real estate agent whose picture has a little haze around it because it was shot in the eighties when she wasn't sure if she was going to go into the adult movie industry or be a realtor? And yet she's still using that same picture today, even though she's forty years older. The real estate industry is rife with this practice.

I bring this up almost every time I speak at a real estate convention, and while everyone laughs, they know that most of the people in the audience are doing exactly that. They're focusing on what they look like.

When I was looking to purchase my current house, I saw a flier of the agent that was selling it, and she looked to be in her forties. When she turned up? She looked about sixty-five. Now, I could care less what she looked like. I wanted someone who would find me my forever home, a place that would be comfortable for me, my dogs, my wife, and my kids (in that order). I wanted a solution to my problem—but she felt it was more important to focus on what she looked like in a picture, as if that had anything to do with whether or not I bought a house. I don't know anyone who has purchased a home because the agent was hot or didn't because they were ugly. (Please send all your sexist comments on this topic to dontcare@stevedsims.com.)

She was focused on herself when she should have been focused on her clients. We met for the first time at a house she was showing me, and when she got out of the car, I felt conned. Now, she turned out to be a lovely woman, and she did end up selling me my beautiful home, but the first moment I met her, I felt as if she was a fraud who had lied to me. That is not a good anchor for the beginning of a relationship. You don't want your customer's first thought to be, *I've just been lied to. What else does she lie about?*

Why have we, as a society, decided that this is the world we want to live in? We need to focus on the substance. Another bad example of this trend is in our videos. Our attention span has dramatically decreased in recent years. In my generation, we used to speak to someone for at least ten to fifteen minutes before we decided if we wanted to get to know them better. Today, you have ten seconds at most before the person you're speaking to has made a decision on whether they like you or not. So what do we do? We make videos.

Personally, I love making videos because I've never spelt a word wrong while making one. More seriously, videos give you a chance to not only talk about whatever your topic is, but to also engage your viewers' eyeballs with your smile, your passion, and your tonality.

Tonality is extremely hard to put into text. If I text you *Let's get a beer tomorrow at 8 p.m.* and you're in a bad mood, you're going to read that as an order or as if I'm trying to control you. You're going to think, *I'm not bound to him,* and respond back, *9 p.m.* But, if you're in a good mood, you're going to agree enthusiastically to eight o'clock.

When it comes to tonality in text, it's not about what you write but how it's read. In a video, you get to remove that layer of confusion because you can see the enthusiasm and excitement of the speaker.

In today's economy, people are creating more videos for their businesses (and if you're not, you should), but understand: those videos are not about you. Don't spend four hours doing your hair to give a bad message. Get your phone out, think: what am I about to say, what am I about to show them, what do I need to teach them? Can that help them?

Don't worry about vanity metrics, either. You don't need four million followers because you can't take on four million clients.

After I spoke at a chiropractor event, one of the doctors came up to me and said, "I do a lot of videos, and I want to get them to go viral. Can you help me?"

I challenged him and asked, "Why?"

"I want more people to see what I do."

Again: "Why?"

"Well, right now, my videos are only giving me about 60,000 views."

I said, "That's great. So what are you looking for?" Again, I was challenging the why in order to find out what he really wanted.

"I want more clients."

At this point, I was confused. "Let me get this straight. You have 60,000 people watching your videos, but your client book isn't packed? Sounds to me like you're talking to the wrong people. What's your number?"

"What do you mean by my number?"

"Give me your number in your business. What's your number?"

"Well, I'm trying to get to two million followers," he started.

"No," I said. "I already explained you're getting the wrong eyeballs. What's your number? How many clients do you want to book?"

A light bulb went on over his head. "Twenty."

"Great. I'm going to wave my magic wand, and next morning at nine o'clock, twenty Grade A, best-of-the-best clients are going to walk through your door and ask you to look after them. Can you take them on?"

He looked shocked, "No."

"But you said you wanted twenty."

"Yeah, but that's too much."

I talked him down through the numbers until we landed at four. Now we knew what his number was—not two million followers, but four clients. Once you know what your number is, then your focus can be on how to reach them.

Don't pretend to be someone you're not—prettier, smarter, younger—because, again, it's not about you. It's about them. That's what entrepreneurs need to focus on in today's economy. The number one response kids are giving to the question "What do you want to be when you grow up?" is now influencer. That is a clear statement on what we are doing wrong as a generation. There are a lot of successful influencers who have been able to milk the system (case in point, the Kardashians being famous for being famous) and get paid from ads and endorsements, but this won't last forever. It's a blip.

We need to focus on the substance. Stop worrying about what you look like. The right customer isn't going to care about your hair or your age or your clothes. They aren't trying to date you. They want you to solve their problem. When you start focusing on being the solution, you can walk on stages, create videos, and produce educational courses because everything you are making reflects on how you care about the people you are communicating to, instead of how big your butt looks in those jeans.

FOCUS ON THE CONNECTION

Stop focusing on views, followers, and likes, and start focusing on communication, clients, and—the most important c word—connection.

If you don't want to be Amazonified, you need to focus on connecting a person with a problem with your solution. If you don't challenge yourself to connect with people, you aren't going to stay in business.

Now, I get it; we all want to look the best we can, but looking good is focusing on you and failing on connection. A good friend of mine, Joe Polish, once told me, "There's a difference between being easy to understand and impossible to misunderstand." When he said that line to me, it shook me. It was very, very powerful. I realised that the reason I get so much business is because I'm impossible to misunderstand.

So many people dislike me because I make it very easy for them to make that choice, which is great for me and them. The worst thing that could happen is to discover that you don't resonate with the person you've spent the last six months talking to. You want to make sure that decision is made as soon as possible.

There are three kinds of people on the planet. The first are the people that love you no matter what you say. You walk in the room, and they like the colour of your sunglasses, the look of your earrings. They think your accent is charming. The second group of people are the ones that want nothing to do with you. "I don't trust him. I don't like him. I don't connect with him."

Both of these groups are wonderful. They're the people you want to deal with because it makes it easier for you to always know where you stand. Neither you nor they are wasting time.

There's a third group of people, however, and they are the worst—but they're your fault. They are the fence-sitters. They're the people hovering nearby saying, "I'm not sure what this guy's trying to say. I'm not sure I'm fully getting this. There's something that's not quite right." We've all had these feelings when we first meet someone. But I don't want you to have that feeling when you meet me. I want to be transparent enough that you can make a decision quickly on whether or not you want to stay in this conversation.

At a big event a few weeks ago, there were about twenty tables to choose from to sit at while the speakers were talking. I picked a table, and about five minutes in, I realised there were three people at this table that I was not going to be able to connect with. I didn't want to be rude to the speakers on stage, so I waited for a coffee break and then moved to another table.

At that table, there was one person there I didn't like, and he got louder the longer the event went on. So again, I moved to another table, and this one was perfect. It took me two tables, but by lunchtime, I was at a table that I could stay at for the next day and a half. My standards didn't let me accept anything less. (See how everything is coming together? I wasn't afraid to look stupid moving tables because my standards told me that I deserved to be at a table where I could form relationships with my tablemates.)

You see, you have to focus on making sure you are impossible to misunderstand in order for people to be able to connect with you and for you to be able to make sure that you are working an actual ROE.

An ROI is a Return on Investment. ROE is a Return on Effort.

Imagine you have to make ten phone calls to ten clients you don't really like. Two things are going to happen. First, you're going to avoid making those phone calls. What should take two or three days is going to take you two weeks to make eight calls. And you'll keep finding reasons to not make those last two calls. Second, you're going to be miserable after you've made the first two or three calls because you're only dealing with people you don't like. It's sapping your energy and taking the joy out of your soul while you sit there saying, "No, no, no." "I understand." "Yes, yes. You're right." Over, and over, and over.

How much energy do you lose when you have to make ten phone calls to ten people you love? Again, two things are going to happen. First, those calls are still going to take you two weeks, but this time, it's because you won't shut up. You'll get on the phone and have a great conversation, and before you know it, the day is half over. Second, you are going to be smiling at the end of every phone call. You're going to be regenerated.

The Return on Effort when you speak to someone you don't like is bad. You're tired, disgruntled, you're barking at the people around you. When your wife asks you how your day was, you'll snap back at her, "Oh, what do you care?" You're in a bad mood, and you spread the cancer of a bad connection to everyone around you.

When you're in a good mood, you regenerate. It's like you have solar panels on your body, and the conversation was the sun that filled them with electricity. You're riding high on energy from the conversations that were easy to have. After all, how hard is it for you to have a conversation with your best friend? It's not.

But for most conversations, you spend time and energy putting up armour to pretend to be someone you're not. This armour removes the ability for someone you meet to connect with the real you because you're so focused on saying, "Here's the key for my Ferrari." "This suit was custom made for me."

While you were so focused on your looks and your armour, this guy with his black t-shirt and black jeans who pulled up on a motorcycle and walked in with a helmet under his arm walked out with a $2 million deal because he focused on the person's problem and being the solution.

I'm just one example of someone who became the solution

and dared to go for stupid. The world is full of examples of people who chose to turn left when everyone was shouting at them to go right.

GO FOR STUPID

Ask yourself these three questions and answer them in the space below.

1. How current is your profile picture?

....

2. Do your social pages depict the real you or who you want people to think you are?

....

3. Do you show up as you or who you want people to meet?

....

CHAPTER ELEVEN

GOING FOR STUPID: IT'S NOTHING NEW

All throughout this book, we've talked about getting into a mindset where you dare to go for stupid ideas and goals, where you start stupid and achieve ridiculous. I'd love to claim this is a brand-new idea, but the truth is, throughout history there are examples where someone was told, "That will never work," and they went ahead and did it anyway to wild success.

This chapter brings you the origin story of some common items we use in everyday life—items without which life would be worse—that we only have because someone dared to go for stupid.

LET THERE BE LIGHT

Imagine it's the middle of winter, and you started reading this amazing book by a British bricklayer that you can't put down. You sit by the window reading all afternoon, but then the sun goes down at 4:30 p.m., and with it, you lose your reading light.

What do you do? Turn on the lamp and turn the page.

Everyone knows that Thomas Edison developed the first electric light bulb (no, we're not getting into patent theft here). What you may not know is that most people, including intelligent ones, thought it was a stupid idea. One person said that it was "unworthy of the attention of practical or scientific men," while another said it was a sham.

Where would we be today if Thomas Edison had listened to these critics? The world would be a lot darker, that's for sure.

RING, RING

In a moment that changed history, Alexander Graham Bell created and patented the first telephone. However, when he went to sell this incredible new invention, investors laughed. They said it would never amount to anything more than an expensive toy.

Bell took their laughter as a sign to forge ahead and founded his own company to mass produce his invention. By the late 1880s, there were tens of thousands of landline telephones across the country.

WHAT'S ON THE TELLY?

Radio talent scoffed when the first television was revealed in

1926. They said it would never take off, it would be too expensive to make, and was a waste of time and thought.

Twenty years later, in the late 1940s, people still didn't think television would take off. Who would want to stare at a box all night? TV manufacturers and show producers ignored the contempt and continued to innovate. Today, almost every home in the world has at least one television set—and movies and TV shows make trillions of dollars a year.

IT'S FOR THE BIRDS

You probably already know the Wright Brothers built and flew the first plane in 1903. What you might not know is that one of the brothers, Wilbur, had said in 1901 that it would take fifty years for man to be able to fly. He ridiculed *himself*. Yet two years later, he was making history, proving sometimes you have to ignore laughter coming from yourself too.

Even once the first planes were made and successfully flying, there were still naysayers laughing at them. One military commander even said that planes would never be useful for the military. Can you imagine what military defence would be like if manufacturers had shrugged and given up on the idea of long-flight, ammo-filled planes?

CARS

In the early 1900s, cars were begrudgingly accepted as a luxury item for the wealthy. It would never be used by the common people, even if prices eventually dropped, and certainly never used as often as the human-powered bicycle.

Cars were called a fad, a novelty, a whim. Horses would continue to be the only way to travel long distances, and bikes would get you around town. Henry Ford ignored everyone who thought his idea was stupid, and by 1918, over half of the cars on the road were Model Ts.

TELL THAT TO ELON!

While people could wrap their heads around the idea of sending a machine to space, they drew the line at a rocket manned by humans going to space. The contempt for spacecraft was thick, with one person saying human space travel would never happen no matter what technology was created and another saying that there was no way any machine could leave our atmosphere.

Rocket scientists didn't care what anyone said or thought. They knew it was possible, and in 1961, Yuri Gagarin, a Russian astronaut, became the first human to go to space, starting a race that's still alive today.

THE WORLD AT YOUR FINGERTIPS

Could you do your job without a computer? Odds are the answer is no. After the first computer was invented and presented to the world, naysayers said that it was as far as the computer could go—we'd never do better.

Of course, computer enthusiasts paid no attention to them and continued to make great advances. But with every advancement, the naysayers got louder. They didn't believe that any regular person would ever want a computer at home.

Today, almost every American owns or has regular access to a computer.

ADD TO CART

Online shopping was a saving grace during the pandemic for me and millions of others trapped in their homes. However, when it was first created, no one thought it would take off. After all, some people believed "Women need to get out of their house," and shopping was the perfect opportunity. Now, online shopping is the most popular way to shop.

A COMPUTER IN YOUR POCKET

People didn't have great reactions to the first landline telephones, so you won't be surprised to find out that they didn't have great reactions to the first mobile phone either. This is another example of even the creator of an invention laughing at themself. In the 1980s, a high-level employee at Motorola who had helped create one of the very first cell phones predicted that they would never take the place of landline phones. Now you can look that quote up on your cell phone.

HAVE YOU HEARD OF STARBUCKS?

I refuse to start my day without my cappuccino. Judging by the number of coffee shops in Beverly Hills alone, I'm not the only one who relies on the drink.

However, the big thinkers of the 1500s disagreed. They tried to stop the drink from becoming popular for a variety of reasons:

it produced a form of drunkenness, coffeehouses encouraged reactionaries, and that it was causing common diseases.

Thankfully, they were unsuccessful because the coffeehouse owners refused to back down. They knew they had a good thing going, and they were successful in making coffee a required drink for almost every person on the planet.

DON'T RAIN ON MY PARADE

Rain wasn't the only thing the first umbrella user in Britain had to shield himself from. When Jonas Hanway brought an umbrella back from France, people thought he was a dandy as parasols were clearly only used to protect delicate females from the sun.

Unconcerned, he continued using his umbrella every time it rained (which, in Britain, is a lot) to keep himself dry—and to block the trash people threw at him. It would take several more decades for the English population to finally accept that it would be great to have an object that kept them dry 90 per cent of the year.

All of these people refused to stay stationary, even when life was good, but especially when it was not. They tried and tried again. They avoided being the same person every day—they continued to grow through failure.

THEIR KODAK MOMENT

Did you know that Kodak invented the first digital camera? They created it as a test and even made and sold a prototype. However, they quickly abandoned it as a fad. The team thought that digital cameras were just a gimmick. I bet years later, some of those executives wished they had ignored the giggles when digital cameras became a mainstream, coveted product that eventually put Kodak out of business.

When you are creating your business plan, and people attempt to trivialise or laugh at it, you need to decide: is this your Kodak moment? Will you choose to abandon your idea and move on to the next shiny object? If so, be prepared to be put out of business one day by someone who ignored the laughs.

GO FOR STUPID

Ask yourself these three questions and answer them in the space below.

1. What is something you do that others may consider stupid but that you know works?

....

2. What's happened in your industry that was first viewed as stupid but is now commonplace?

....

3. What is a stupid experience that you dare yourself to achieve?

....

CHAPTER TWELVE

CHALLENGE THEIR WHY

On what turned out to be our last night out before lockdown in 2020, we went to a Mexican restaurant. When we got home, we turned on the news to hear that at midnight, everything was being closed, and everyone needed to stay home. I was mortified that my last meal had been at a rather poor restaurant in LA. If I had known I wouldn't be able to eat out for two years, I would have picked somewhere far greater.

The next morning, there was pandemonium, confusion, and aggression all over social media. There were comments saying, "This is all politics." "It's not really here." "It's made up." Everyone was venting.

However, a few of the people I was communicating with were asking, "What are we going to do with this time we've been given?" You see, no one knew how long this was going to last:

four days, four weeks, four months, a year? There was no way of knowing—and that was the problem.

I noticed that the panic people were experiencing was because they didn't have an end date. If we had known from the first day of lockdown that it was going to end on June 1, 2021, people would have allocated their time accordingly. "Time for me to work on my garden!" "I can finally learn Spanish." "Let me perfect how to make the Christmas cake."

We didn't have that clear end date. We were in a state of confusion, noise, and distraction. And it created a lot of controversy. I chose to follow the advice of Dr. Sean Stephenson that we talked about way back in Chapter Two: "Was this done to me or for me?" I decided this was done for me.

I wanted to see how I could make this lockdown benefit me. The first thing I noticed was that COVID removed a lot of the tasks in my life that I didn't want to be involved in. I love speaking. I love being in a new location, immersing myself in different cultures and meeting new people. I don't, however, like the travel aspect of it. I don't like getting on a plane to fly there, I don't like packing, and I don't like the unpacking. If you want to spend a week in Italy, you know that you're going to lose two of those days to travel. Plus, it's exhausting.

With the lockdown, people no longer had to travel, even for everyday tasks. They were saving themselves two to three hours a day. We were given more time, something that we have always desperately wanted. When I came to this realisation—that I had been handed more time gift-wrapped with a giant bow on the top—I needed to figure out how I could maximise it.

I started focusing internally on my messaging. Looking at the messaging that companies were putting out, I saw a confused world thanks to a lack of clarity. I wondered if I was being unclear to the people I was working with and marketing to. I wanted to make sure that I was impossible to misunderstand.

I had already been pretty clear, but I was far from perfect, so I went through my social feeds and looked for anything that needed updating. For instance, I found some pictures that hadn't been updated, including one of me from ten years ago when I was slimmer.

I realised I had lost continuity while I was on the speeding train of life. Thank you, COVID—yes, I'm saying it—for giving me the time to be able to look into the mirror, at my messaging, and at my business. In fact, the most successful people used COVID as a time to impact their life. I was able to update my website, social feeds, copy, email campaigns, newsletters, and blogs: me in the digital world. I removed all confusion and installed clarity in its place.

My son was using the time to do the same thing with his business, which handled backend marketing, SEO, and retargeting programs. While we were chatting about what we were updating, we had a realisation.

I knew a lot about branding because I have worked with some of the biggest companies and brands on the planet. If I knew how to make branding work for me, could I translate that knowledge to work for someone else? The only way to find out was to try it.

SIMS.MEDIA WAS BORN

I contacted a few friends (start small) and said, “Hey! I noticed a few things when I was updating my branding, and I noticed you share the same problem. Would you be interested in working with me to amplify your voice, tone, following, niche, and business in what’s being called the worst period of our life? Can I help you?”

A few of them said yes, so I worked on their branding, while my son, Henry, worked on their marketing. We removed the confusion, increased the clarity, and made sure their potential customers understood what problem their company had the solution to.

It was so successful we decided to launch an official business together: Sims.Media. Since its creation at the start of the pandemic in 2020, Sims.Media has worked with over seventy clients and built over a hundred new websites. We’ve revamped coaches, influencers, and anyone else who needed personal branding.

From this venture, we’ve noticed that the world is easy to understand when you split it into two boxes: the world of conversation today and knowing purchase power is either aspirational- or solution-based.

One of the most beautiful things about solving a problem is that nine times out of ten when you are removing someone’s pain, they don’t care what you look like. Remember the headache tablet logo example? When you solve someone’s problem, it’s all about them. You don’t need to have a pretty website. You don’t have to look like a supermodel in a bikini. None of that is relevant.

On the aspirational side, the two most commonly seen industries are watches and cars. Let's look at a car advert as an example. Almost every time you see a commercial or ad for a car, you see a pair of hands on the steering wheel. Why? Because that ad is placing *you* in the driver's seat. As the commercial continues, the camera pans off the steering wheel and over to the passenger seat, where there's a beautiful person staring adoringly at you.

It makes the viewer think, *If I get this car, I can get that relationship and that life and live in eternal sunshine.* I have never seen a car advert with a fat person driving through rainy, congested London. They're always gliding down the Pacific Coast Highway or through the Italian hillside to trigger you into a dream state where you want that item to get that life.

Watches are similar. "When you've made it." That was the copy on an old Rolex advert. I'll be blunt: Rolex makes gorgeous watches, but not a single one of those watches is ever going to outperform a $299 Apple Watch, or your phone, or honestly, the cheapest digital watch from Walmart or the local gas station. They are all going to tell time just as well as any kind of high-end Swiss watch, and with a much better price tag than $50,000–100,000.

But it's aspirational. You purchase a Rolex watch as a statement to who you are, where you fit, and what your standards are without having to say a single word to the person you are communicating with.

QUESTIONS FOR THE OWNERS

The first question business owners have to ask themselves before they can come up with a stupid goal and scale to ridiculous is "Am I a solution or am I aspiration?" Only then can you understand the conversations you need to have. You don't converse about an aspirational product in the same tonality that you do if you are providing a solution.

Once you know your standpoint, you need to know where you are having the conversation. Looking back only five years ago, the biggest platform people consumed media on was television. In fact, it made up about 70 per cent of media consumption, with the rest divided between the internet and radio. Since the early 2020s, 85 per cent of our media has been consumed through our phones.

When parents sent their kids to college in the 2000s, they'd buy them a TV. Now, more "TV" is consumed by tablets, phones, and computers than they are by an actual TV. Kids live and die with their phones. If you take a teenager's phone away, they act as if you've removed a limb. They enter panic mode.

Not too long ago, a report was sent to me by one of my team members, and originally, I questioned its legitimacy because it seemed too ridiculous to be true. It stated that, on average, teenagers spend more time talking to AI than they do to their best friend. I thought, *That can't be true. That's a stretch. My boy is always on the phone talking to his mates.* But then, I considered it more. The majority of the time, he's not verbally talking to them, he's texting them. Yet he's always telling Alexa and Siri to do things for him.

Those may only be three- to five-second quotes each time, but added together, they turn into hundreds of hours in a year. Yet he'd only verbally talk to his friends in short bursts that totalled an hour every few weeks.

This fact is terrifying because it's data-based proof that humans, especially the younger generations who have never known anything else, are losing the ability to communicate because everything they do is transactional.

Think about going through McDonald's.

"Can I help you?"

"Yeah, I want a number six, large, no pickles, with a Diet Coke."

"That'll be $7.89. Please pull around."

That's it. That's the entire conversation—or should I say transaction.

On Amazon, it's click to add to cart. "Hey, Siri, turn off the lights." "Alexa, lower the temperature."

Think about the last time you went to a website and had a question. Instead of phoning the company, you probably clicked the chat button in the bottom corner and were met with a response such as *Hi! My name's Susie. I'm an automated receptionist. How can I help you?* followed by a list of static topics to choose from.

Companies are bringing in AI under the guise that it helps

customers, but it actually increases their bottom line. Chat bot software is generally a one-time purchase—purchase, install, add some answers, and finish.

The good news for customers is that AI is getting smarter and smarter every year. Peter Diamandis, founder of the XPI and 360, says that every five years, AI learns about ten times more than a human brain, and it will be able to think, analyse, and estimate faster than a human brain before we've hit 2030.

This means it won't be long before AI is smarter than us. At the moment, it's trying to recognise and replicate, with varying levels of success. But every time you speak to an AI using slang—"Hey, dude"—it learns how to be more natural.

The challenge we face is bringing the art of communication back to these mobile platforms where people are consuming conversation. That's why, before you send a message to anyone, you have to ask yourself, "How is the person I'm talking to more liable to receive that message?"

If you write a long, scrolling message into an email and send it to someone with a big computer screen, that may be easy to digest. But if you take all of that information and send it through text, you're actually sending them information overload. What do they do? Read the first two sentences (if you're lucky), give up, and ignore it.

You need to understand where the person you want to have a conversation with is going to consume the conversation. Let me be blunt: the possibility of you achieving anything stupid, fantastical, or amazing comes down to your ability to be able to communicate your goal.

It's also important to remember that no matter how you send your message, your mood when you send it is irrelevant. It's 100 per cent dependent on the mood of the receiver when they receive it. Think back to our beer example from Chapter Ten. If you text your mate, *Beer. Tomorrow night. 8 p.m. Be there.* and they're in a good mood when they read it, they'll think *Fantastic!* because they transposed their happy mood onto your words. But if they're in a foul mood because their best friend just ran away with their girlfriend, they're going to transpose their bad mood onto your words. Now it sounds like you are ordering them around, and they're going to push back.

We need to focus on the mood of the recipients. But because we can't predict the life and mood of every single person who sees our videos or reads our posts online, we need to ensure that every message we send is impossible to misunderstand. Brevity is king—keep it short, keep it clear. Every conversation you have, you need to ask yourself, *Could this be misconstrued? Could this be read as a negative, a challenge, or an order? Can this be seen in a bad light in any way, shape, or form?* When the answer is no, that's when you hit send (or post or upload).

You might be asking yourself, "Steve, why are we talking about communication?" The answer to that is I believe that everything is about communication. My first book, *Bluefishing: The Art of Making Things Happen*, is about communication. This book: communication. The success of everything you do today is based on your ability to communicate your goals with yourself, with your team, and with your audience. Learn how to do it right.

CHALLENGE YOUR CLIENT

Communication is when two people actually talk about a problem they have. If you answer someone's problem with what they asked for, that's not communication, that's a transaction. You need to bring out your inner Sherlock and challenge the person you see.

My favourite word is one that some people believe to be the most offensive word in the dictionary: why. (If you want to know why you need to ask why three times, read *Bluefishing*. There's a whole section dedicated to it.) You need to challenge people to understand what they actually want versus what they're saying.

Here's an example for you. This takes us back to when I worked with Elton John on his Oscar party. Someone contacted me because they knew that I was involved in the party and told me that they wanted to meet Elton. I said, "Oh, that's great. Why?"

It was a simple, one-word question because I wanted to understand why he wanted to meet Elton John. He said, in a very, very arrogant tone, "Well, he's one of the last living legends. I don't know how long he's going to be alive, and I want to get a picture that I can stick on my desk. Can you make that happen?"

I was confused about the statement on how long he's going to live. It made me wonder if he knew something that I didn't, and it was concerning. So I said, "Oh, that's great. Let me see what I can do, and I'll come back to you." But I didn't come back to it. I didn't want any part of that. His why was shallow; there was no substance. I couldn't have formed a relationship with this man based on the fact that all he wanted was a photograph to stick on his desk.

A month later, I received another phone call that was first picked up by someone on my team. She stepped into my office and said, "I have this guy on the phone who wants to meet Elton John. It sounds like the guy you told us about. I think he's following up?"

I said, "I'll take it." But when I picked up the phone, it turned out to be a different person. He also wanted to get a photograph with Elton John, so I asked him the same question: why? He got quiet for a moment and then said, "My dad used to drive me to and pick me up from school. That was our thing. It was never my mom—always my dad, there and back. My dad's first car had this jammed cassette in it, and it was Elton John's *Greatest Hits*. It was the only thing that the car could play. We never could get that cassette out. When he sold the car, it went with the cassette.

"Every day on the way to school, we'd play that Elton John cassette and sing our lungs out. Then, when he picked me up after school, we'd hit start and sing our lungs out on the way home. When he bought a new car, it had a CD player in it. And the first CD he ever bought was Elton John's *Greatest Hits* so we could sing our lungs out again.

"I remember hitting high school and hating the fact that he

would pull up singing his lungs out. I would jump in the car and slam the door so fast and try to sink into the chair so no one could see or hear my dad sing his lungs out. I used to moan to my mom about it, but she found it funny. My dad found it funny too. Then I got my own car, and I never had to put up with him singing Elton John on the way to school. I drove in peace with no fear of embarrassment. I thought these were very happy moments of my life."

He got quiet again for a few moments and took a shaky breath. "My dad died about ten years ago, and I have kids myself now. I'll be driving down the road listening to the radio, and Elton John will come on. And for the next three minutes, my dad is next to me again, singing his lungs out. Random moments throughout my life, Elton John brings my father back to sing with me. I want to tell him that, and I want to thank him for keeping my dad alive."

That was his why—and it was a good one. I arranged for him to come to the party, and he told Elton John his story. The party was loud, so I couldn't hear what they were saying, but I could see them both well up as the story went on, and when it was over, they hugged. They took a photograph together, and it was a beautiful moment—one I was able to get because I dared to challenge the client for their why.

Don't take what a person is asking for on their words alone. Dare to have a conversation, dare to have a relationship, and dare to have a connection by challenging the person's question. "Why is that important? How can I help you? Should we be looking at something else like this instead?"

Make sure you never become a transaction. Avoid Amazonification and enter into a relationship.

GO FOR STUPID

Ask yourself these three questions and answer them in the space below.

1. What are you going to do in the next three months so you're not the same person in six months?

....

2. How are you going to commit to challenging your clients' requests with why?

....

3. How confusing are you to your prospects?

....

CONCLUSION

Since birth, I have been both aggravated and curious, which is quite the Molotov cocktail of emotions. And when you're eighteen years old, riding around on a motorcycle, covered in tattoos and piercings, it doesn't always lead you down the right path. But my wife showed me that my aggravation, married with my curiosity, has propelled me forward my entire life.

As kids get older, adults dilute them. We tell them it's time to grow up, stop fantasising, and stop dreaming. But aren't those the cornerstones of creativity?

When I was growing up, I never said, "I want to do this." I always asked, "Why can't I do this?" That mindset led me to constantly challenge myself to grow as a person. In fact, I'll go so far as to say I would be mortified to find that in six months' time, I was the same person I am today.

Don't mistake me. I have a very nice life. I'm happy, secure, and confident in my family, my friends, my relationships, and my businesses—all the areas you should constantly check in on. But I always want more. I want to push myself to see what I'm capable of. I want to experience everything I can.

This doesn't mean I'm going to run down to Vegas and bet my house on black. It means that when I'm in a sushi restaurant, I'm going to try something I've never tried before. I'll go see a movie that I barely understand the concept of but that I want to experience.

The more you try, the more those experiences stretch the elastic band of your mindset and give you a greater opportunity to receive.

My family has a ritual to expand our horizons. Every time we go to a restaurant as a family, we order something on the menu that we've never had before. When you're in an American restaurant, you mostly recognise everything on the menu, so it doesn't get too wild. When you're in a sushi restaurant, it can sometimes turn out quite horrific. We don't always recognise a lot of the items on the menu, so we guess what something is and order it. Usually, we do this with the appetiser. For $5, you get to gamble on whether what you ordered is the greatest thing you've ever tasted or the thing that makes you say, "Oh my God, why did that enter my mouth?"

My kids always complained when they were younger: "Why do we always have to do this?" Now that they're grown, they argue over who gets to be the person to order the new item.

GROWTH COMES FROM THE ATTEMPT

Your growth doesn't come from success. You don't grow because you achieved something. Growth only comes when you attempt something new and, quite often, when that new thing you attempted doesn't go well. Remember, failure is an education in what not to do.

Your Facebook advertising could tank. Your newsletter could have gone out with the design messed up. Your book could have gone to print with typos in it. Today, I am an exceptionally competent, confident, and well-paid international speaker because I learned from the terrible, horrible, no-good speeches I gave when I first started out. My wife has always said that I'm a fifty-five-year-old five-year-old.

I dare you to be that five-year-old who refused to be diluted. Keep dreaming, keep fantasising, keep imaging, and stay curious enough that you'll dare to open the box you were told not to. Try that podcast that everyone laughed at the idea of. Try the new marketing idea even though no one else can understand what you're talking about. Dare to try. Dare to stretch your horizons. Dare to challenge yourself to risk failure, which is the only way that growth can happen.

Remember, when you fail at something, you become educated on what didn't work. Education leads to experience. Experience leads to credibility. Credibility is something that you can invoice.

That is the trajectory of growth. I want to be someone who is constantly growing because if you aren't growing, you become stagnant. And when you're stagnant, you begin to sink. Once you begin to sink, you're done.

I don't ever want to be stagnant, so I stay in constant motion. I'll share a secret with you. When I started writing this book, it was scary, horrible, intimidating, and very uncomfortable. It was something I would rather have not done. But I wasn't doing it for the money, which is why I could push through those hard feelings. I wrote this book for the impact on you, the reader, and for the people I end up coaching because of it, the people I speak to on stage, and the people who live on the opposite side of the planet who realise *If that guy's doing it, I'm already out of excuses.*

This impact is why I was willing to grow and write this book, even in the worst moments of fear and discomfort. As a good friend once told me, "You have to be comfortable with being uncomfortable."

LAST WORDS

I want to leave you with my favourite quote from a good friend of mine:

"The first time you try anything, it will be shit. Get going, then focus on getting good!"

Thank you for reading this book. Thank you for being aggravated enough to demand more of yourself.

Please leave a review on Amazon, and make sure to look me up at www.stevedsims.com or @stevedsims anywhere you consume social media (Instagram, Twitter, etc.). I'm the same name on all of them (and why wouldn't I be? I am Steve D. Sims, after all).

ACKNOWLEDGMENTS

How do I acknowledge everyone in my life who gave me massive deals and introductions—or the relationships who gave me those relationships?

As my friend Joe Polish says, "It's dominos. Who was the first, who was the most important? That's a tough one."

I can say that I'm nothing without those around me. To list many of them would mean excluding even more, so simply put: if we know each other and we call ourselves friends, then I owe you a great deal of thanks.

Thanks.

EBD 13696
28-8-25